WHISKEY COWBOY

A Foster House Novella

WALKER ROSE

LE Publishing

 Formatted with Vellum

The woman I spent one hot night with ends up being my boss's daughter, and if I want to keep my job, I won't touch her again.

I work with my two brothers on Hawthorne Guest Ranch. We do the behind-the-scenes stuff with the real ranch and have strict orders to stay away from the guests, the staff, and especially the boss's daughters. I do what I'm told, but when a woman comes into the bar and says she's passing through, well... I give her a night to remember and try not to think about how I'd like to see her again.

I do see her again. The very next day, when she's introduced not only as Jamison Hawthorne, but our newest staff member.

I try to stay away from her, but she has a way of making a guy want more. Only I don't have more to give her. All that's in my name is an old mine some whiskey CEO wants to turn into his next distillery. Yet if I keep sneaking around with Jamison, I'll lose my job and get my brothers fired too. So it's up to me to figure out how to be more for Jamison than some whiskey cowboy.

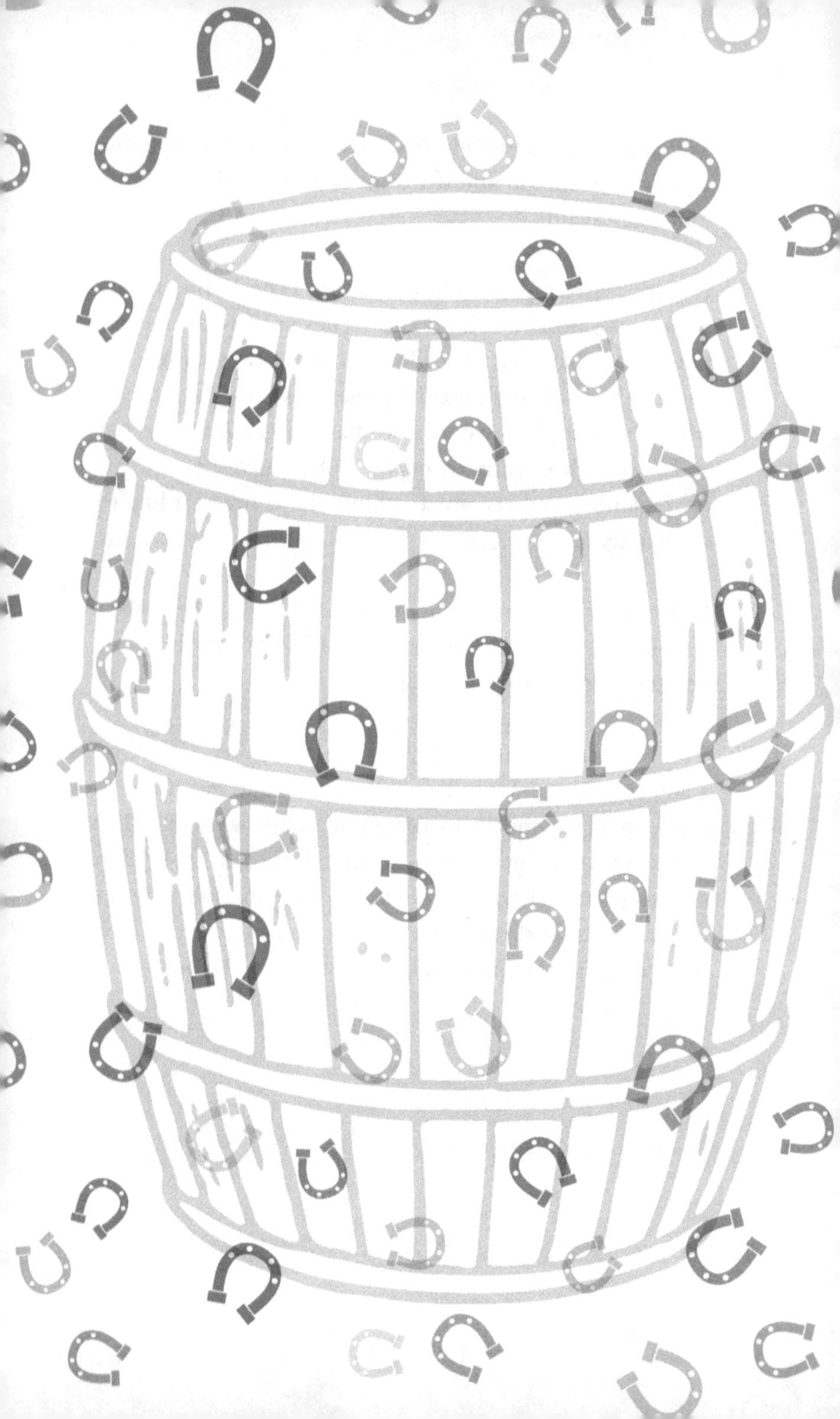

CHAPTER ONE

Iverson

The man sitting across from me looks as out of place as a fish in a cow pen. Neon signs surround us, along with wood-paneled walls and a grungy wood floor. Nothing about Bootleg Tavern is refined. It's old and worn and destined for the rough and rowdy. Myles Foster came dressed for business.

When I knew him, he wasn't wearing black slacks with a crease, loafers that are probably expensive as hell, and a gray dress shirt. He resembled me. Plain T-shirt, worn jeans, cowboy boots, and a shitty attitude.

The attitude is the same.

"I'm not selling," I say and take a drink of my whiskey.

The tract of land with an old gold mine my dad left to me and my two younger brothers is all we have left of him, all that the Hennessy name is known for. I take another pull of my whiskey and let the charred oak and vanilla flavor play over my tongue. He drove all the way to Huckleberry Springs, Montana, for nothing. He can find some other abandoned land to buy for his new distillery.

"Think on it, Iverson." Myles taps the bar top and points to my drink. "You ordered Foster House. You can be part of the story."

I snort. What story? He got rich making whiskey. I'm a hired ranch hand. Where do I fit in? "It's not just me. It's my brothers too."

"Selling it will do a lot more for you than what it's doing now."

"Not if you don't know any more good fishing spots."

"That can be arranged."

Silas, the older bartender, stops in front of us, his wary gaze on Myles. "What can I getcha?"

Myles puts a couple of twenties on the table. "I'll have what he's having. Put his on my tab."

Silas grunts and swaggers away, the old rodeo injury he likes to tell us about every weekend putting a hitch in his stride.

"You and your brothers will come out of the deal very nicely," Myles says.

Not that nice. Myles can't replace the only good memories Haven, Durban, and I have of growing up. "I'm not selling out." I take a drink. Damn, he makes good whiskey. It'd be easier to say no if he made cheap shit. "Besides—Huckleberry Springs is a bit far from Denver, isn't it?"

This little town is over an hour southwest of Billings. Last I heard, Foster House Whiskey is produced outside of Denver in an old, converted mine. Myles has a type when it comes to where he builds his distilleries.

He folds up the sleeves of his shirt. "I live in Bourbon Canyon now."

Surprise filters through me. We both have history in Bourbon Canyon. I don't think his was much longer than mine, not enough to draw him back.

"Which is why I'm here," he continues. "I married Wynter. Wynter Kerrigan."

I scrub a hand down my face as the name encourages other long-buried memories to the surface. "One of the four adopted girls?"

"Yes. The youngest."

I cock a brow at him. Myles is at least five years older than me, putting him somewhere close to forty-four. He was a teenager in the foster home my brothers and I were shuttled to after our dad went missing. Wynter was even younger than me, as I recall from the short time I was there. "What'd Mae think of that?"

Mae Bailey and her husband, Darin, were a stable point during one of the most unstable parts of my life. I don't like to remember that time period, but Myles's presence brings it all back. So does asking about my dad's land that got left to me and my brothers, with me in charge.

He gives me a smirk. "She was thrilled since Wynter was twenty-eight when we met again."

I shrug. I don't know him, and I didn't keep in contact with him or the Baileys after my brothers and I were hauled out of Bourbon Canyon to live with our mom in Casper, Wyoming. It was a surprise to all three of us to find out she was alive. It was also a shock to realize she was unhinged, and that was why we were living with Dad until he died.

I shake the memories off. Life came full circle. I'm

back in Huckleberry Springs, where I was born and where my life hunting, fishing, and camping ended when Dad went missing and was later found dead.

A glass of whiskey slides in front of Myles. He takes a drink and seems to savor the flavor. He sets his glass down, but I keep my gaze on the amber fluid. How'd a guy who had a life similar to mine get enough money to start a distillery? How'd he make it into a top-shelf product? How did he turn into a businessman who still looks at home in the roughneck bar?

My curiosity gets the best of me. "Don't you get sick of it?" When his dark brows rise in question, I tip my forehead toward his glass. "When you're around it all the time?"

He rolls the liquid around in his glass, studying it. "No. I get more curious. What other flavors can I pull out? What can I add? Have you tried our line of cinnamon whiskey?"

"Isn't that what all the kids drink?" The ranch where I live and work attracts pasture parties and secret camping trips for teens trying to get wasted and have sex. I've flushed enough of them out of the trees and found the cheap bottles of beer and Fireball littering the land.

"That's mass-manufactured shit that uses chemical flavoring." He takes another sip. "We infuse our whiskey with real Ceylon cinnamon. It adds a bold, yet delicate, flavor, and once it hits your tongue, you won't ever drink the fake crap again."

I grunt, but my interest rises until I can't help but ask, "What else do you infuse?"

"Anything I think will sell." He chuffs out a laugh. "I

still have to make money, but I'm not willing to do so at the expense of quality."

"You make a lot of money, judging by the look of you." Even his hair is neatly combed. Not a black strand out of place.

"I do. That's why I'm here. I can pay you more than that tract of land is worth."

"Mining companies have already come sniffing around." The land was stripped long before I was born. Even shortly after Dad was born. My grandparents went broke trying to milk more gold, platinum, and palladium out of the dirt. Could there be more found with modern technology? Maybe. But the natural beauty has been restored, and I like it that way. Haven and Durban do too. "I told them no, and I'm telling you the same."

People always want to profit off what isn't theirs.

He tosses back the rest of his drink. "They're companies only after money. I'm a guy lucky enough to have a company that can pay it forward. If I want to keep doing that, I have to expand."

"I'm a charity case?"

"You're a friend."

"Is that what we are?" Yeah, I'm a cynical bastard. Myles and I didn't have anything to do with each other until he came sniffing around my property.

He stands but pauses with one hand braced on the bar top. "One thing I've learned from Mae—and from Darin when he was alive—is to give a shit about the people who flow through our lives."

That's exactly what my brothers and I used to do. Flow through people's lives. We went to school and worked as kids. As adults, we continue to jump from place to place until we made our way back here. Huckleberry Springs is our home. We found honest work. We've built a stable life. I'm not taking that away from them. "How philanthropic."

"I can be. At Foster House, I give preference to people who've been fosters. Those who know what we've been through."

We. My brothers and I were with the Baileys for three months after our dad died before our mom was located. Three months of morning ranch chores, three meals a day with snacks, and routine. If we stayed longer, Darin told us we could learn some of the work that went into the Copper Summit bourbon distillery they owned. That all went to hell once I walked out the door to follow yet another social worker to an unknown world.

He presses a business card with the trademark Foster House yellow on the trim into my hand. "Think about it. I want to build a second site to expand the spirits we make and utilize more techniques, and I'd like it closer to home. I'd rather work with someone I know to make it happen."

My heart clenches on the word home. He wants to build on my home. "I said no."

"The Old Hennessy Mine," he continues, undaunted. "It's got good bones. I wouldn't tear anything down. Just build it up. Like the Baileys did for us." Then he was gone.

I finish my whiskey, but I don't leave. *The Old Hennessy Mine.* It's what people around town call it. Some townsfolk know me and my brothers are the Hennessy boys found living alone after their dad passed away, but most stay out of our business. Usually because we slam the door in their face. The land is ours, but we'd need money to do anything with it, and three cowboys don't earn the big bucks. To get the funds we'd need, we'd have to sell. Or finance. Fuck, I don't know. I learned how to rope cattle, not invest, and my roping skills have paid me actual money.

Stewing over the meeting with Myles, I think about the mine. Dad used to take us around the structure but never inside. He didn't know how solid it was, and twenty years later, neither do I. The thing is nothing but a liability. I chase kids off my boss's property every other weekend during the summer. It's only a matter of time before someone gets too curious and gets hurt. They might be trespassing, but it'd be on my conscience. My brothers' too.

Silas appears in front of me, his cowboy hat down low. "'Nother? The rich guy left enough to cover it."

"One more, Silas. You can keep the rest."

"I don't need the money, Iverson," he says as he pours more Foster House into my glass. I should've told him I wanted something else. Fuck Myles Foster and his millions of dollars. "If I do, I can sell the silver belt I won in the…"

I tune him out without meaning to, but I've heard this one several times before over the last five years I've been working at Hawthorne Ranch.

William Hawthorne's my boss, and I respect the hell out of that guy. He reminds me of Dad, except he does nothing but work. The guy loves it, and I do too, but Dad balanced his life with recreation. Still, I admire William for having something he's passionate about.

I take a sip and stare at the whiskey inside the glass. How do distilled grains have a vanilla flavor? How does Myles infuse cinnamon? Yeah, I've tried his cinnamon whiskey. It's some of the best alcohol I've ever had.

His offer runs through my head. With all that money split three ways, I could do a lot. I could get my own place instead of living in the bunkhouse with the other Hawthorne Ranch employees.

I work someone else's land instead of my own. Dad put all his assets in a trust, and when I turned twenty-five—well beyond the years of Mom trying to get her hands on it—it became mine and Haven's and Durban's, with me as the executor. I've done nothing with that role.

Haven and Durban claim they aren't interested in selling either. Guilt gnaws at my insides. We could be doing more with it, but what? How? I'm the oldest. I'm supposed to have the answers, but my brothers and I are content.

Or have we become complacent?

A cloud of lilies surrounds me as a woman slides into a seat two stools down. I tuck my chin down and peer at her out of the corner of my eye. I thought I knew all the women in town. But this girl is heads and tails above them all. Long, glossy chestnut hair hangs down her back. The neon lights of the bar reflect off the silky strands covering her bare shoulders. Her sundress—goddamn. I can only catch a glimpse of the long, tanned flesh of her legs without leaning back and leering at her. All I can see beyond her curtain of hair is the delicate slope of her nose and long lashes.

Silas squints at her, and the girl tips her head, arching a brow.

"What can I get you?" he asks with a note of awe in his voice.

So he doesn't know her either.

She sucks in a breath and straightens her shoulders. "Kinky Blue, please."

Her husky voice rolls right into my brain and sticks. I'd hear that voice late at night when I had only myself to get off with.

"What?" Silas asks, insult filling his tone.

Instead of doubling down, she laughs. "It's a vodka."

"Is it blue?"

My lips twitch. It isn't often Silas is shocked, but this girl's drink order does it.

"Yes, in fact it is. Tastes like candy. But I can just have a Malibu Coke."

Silas's lips form a line. "I can do is a plain rum and Coke."

"You don't have Malibu?"

He just shakes his head.

"Rum and Coke it is."

Surprised and a little pleased that she doesn't argue with him about why he doesn't have much selection, I concentrate on my own drink.

A few minutes go by before she turns toward me. "You don't look like the type to order a Kinky Blue."

Damn. A woman who looks like that saying the word kinky to me? If I was taking a drink, I would've choked.

"Just whiskey for me," I say, not wishing to encourage her. I'm nursing my drink after a week of being anxious over Myles's request to meet. A whole lot of fucking would ease the tension too, but I need to straighten myself out first.

I don't have to go out of my way to pick up women, but when they learn I have nothing to offer, they often leave quickly enough. I'm good for a good time. That's it. Usually, I don't mind.

Perhaps I'm raw from the feelings my talk with Myles brought up, but I wish I had more to offer someone like this. A person who comes off as gorgeous and good-natured in the smallest of small-town bars. She's refined, and not just because she's sitting primly with one long, curvy leg crossed over the other with a strappy sandal dangling from her foot.

"I like whiskey too," she says in that voice that's pure sex, "but I wanted something lighter. Summery, you know?"

"Like a beer?" I ask as if that should be an obvious choice in a place like Bootleg Tavern. Silas has the five most popular beers on tap, along with the traditional tequila, rum, vodka, gin, whiskey, and bourbon. There are no umbrellas, little swords, and it's a rare treat for him to throw some peanuts on the bar.

"I haven't had a Miller Lite since my pasture party days." She laughs, and damn, the light tinkling sound goes right for my gut. She's vibrant in a way I haven't seen for a long time. She reminds me of easier times, like when my brothers and I explored the trees and wielded our bear spray at any shadow that moved. "I'm sure if I ordered a Fat Tire, I'd get the same stink eye."

I scan the line of taps with the most common, most commercial beers. Silas likes the originals, and he sticks to what he likes. His patrons learn to like it or make their drinks at home.

Hawthorne Ranch has a fancier bar. Since it's a working ranch, in addition to being a vacation spot that offers its guests a taste of life in the West, my boss caters to their pocketbooks. I work the cattle and stay away from the guests. One warning to me and my brothers that we'd get booted out of Huckleberry Springs is all we needed to stay away from the tourists.

We came too far to get back home, and I'm not ruining it.

"I think you're out of luck," I agree.

She twists toward me, and even though I don't want to start anything tonight, I turn my head. Those legs are too tantalizing to resist. A guy can look. Doesn't mean I'll touch.

First, I have to make sure it's okay to even chat with her.

"You a guest at Hawthorne?" If she says yes, I'm done. I steal one glimpse before she answers. The skirt of her dress rides up her lush thighs even more when she changes her position. A simple brush would push the fabric past her panties and—

I clear my throat and focus on my almost-empty whiskey.

"No," she says. "Not a guest."

Then what's she doing in Huckleberry Springs? I ignore my excitement. If she isn't Hawthorne Ranch clientele, she's not off-limits. Not tonight. "Passing through?"

She smiles at Silas when he slides her rum and Coke in front of her. The heat of her attention is back on me, and I like it way too much. I have a condom in my pocket, begging to be used.

"I don't know yet if I'm passing through or not."

Then I'm definitely not fucking with her. If she stays, she'll move on. I'll see her around with some other guy. Like Andrew at the bank. He just got divorced, and he's a nice guy. He'd go better with Miss What's Her Name than my dusty ass.

"I'm Sunny."

Fitting. She lights up the room. "Nice to meet you." I tip my imaginary hat. It's on the front seat of my pickup. "Iverson."

Her brow arches. "Iverson. That's not a name I've heard before."

"My parents liked to use last names as first names." Might've been the most sane thing my mom did.

She laughs again. I like her laugh. A lot. I like that she does it easily, no inhibitions. I wish I could make her laugh more. "Fair."

She scoots over, and her lily scent grows stronger. I never cared about a girl's perfume, lotion, or whatever product they used, but I could bottle her up. "I'm going to be honest, Iverson."

My interest skyrockets. She goes from light and bubbly to serious, and somehow I find that real fucking attractive. "Yeah?"

"You're hot."

"I've heard." It's probably the cowboy effect. The swagger from being on horseback so much and the rugged aura I've adopted from being outside and working with animals that could crush me all day is catnip. It's the same with my brothers. We all have brown hair, brown eyes, and we're tall. Beyond that, men like Andrew are the ones the girls want to marry. Sure, he's single at the moment, but I give it a year, and he'll be engaged. Hell, I'd marry Andrew if I could. He's a nice guy. He gets benefits at his job instead of bug bites and sunburns.

I'm tired. I have years until retirement, and I'm looking at doing the same thing for...almost thirty more years. Fatigue hangs heavy on my shoulders, yet I'm restless. I love my job, but lately, I've been wondering... Is there more out there?

Christ, I'm becoming a country song. I tip my glass back again. I don't need a third drink, but I could use one more sip.

She leans closer. "You seem like you could ride a girl into the sunset."

The last drop of whiskey catches in my throat, and I sputter.

"You okay there, Iverson?" Silas asks from the opposite end of the bar. "I know the Heimlich, but I might break as many ribs as when I rode Spitfire in the San Antonio rodeo..."

I wave off his concern. "Excuse me?" I heard her wrong. That's all.

"Do you want to have sex?"

I nearly choke again. Hell, yes. "Why?"

"Because I do too, and I don't like playing games."

"Did you come to the Bootleg to get laid?" She doesn't seem like the type. She's not rough around the edges. She's not drooping like surviving each day is such a struggle; only a mutual orgasm can make it better.

She takes a gulp of her drink. "No. But then I saw you and thought it might be a good idea."

It's a hell of an idea.

She might not be passing through. What if I see her again?

My brain and my dick have a quick chat, and they decide not to care. She's not a guest. Therefore, she's not off-limits. I give her one last out. "It might be a bad decision."

She cocks her head, and that silky curtain of hair

slips off her shoulder. My palms itch to run through it, to see if she's soft everywhere. "Will it be, Iverson?"

She asks as if I said yes. As if it's some foregone conclusion that I'll end up inside her tonight. And maybe I need to quit fighting the feeling inside me that wants more. I do want more. But right now, I want this woman. And she's giving herself to me.

I check my watch. "It's only ten, Sunny. We've got a lot of hours until sunrise. Better get started."

Sunny

Iverson tosses his beige cowboy hat in the back seat and loads me into his passenger seat.

Is it a bad idea to go somewhere with a man I just met? Yes.

Do I stop him when he takes off out of the parking lot and heads deeper into the wilder parts of Huckleberry Springs? No.

I've always loved this part of town. It's closer to the mountains. There are steeper dips and turns in the terrain, less ranching, and more wilderness. The trees grow taller and are less bushy, and the Stillwater River cuts through the land, twisting and turning while giving gorgeous glimpses of blue between the green trees.

If it was daylight, I'd have my hand out the window and enjoy the drive. Instead, the knot in my belly cinches tighter. Not out of fear. I might be willfully naive right now because the cowboy next to me looks like he could rope a girl five different ways, and she'd love each and everyone and ask for more. The only dangerous vibe I'm getting is right to the chest.

I've known guys like Iverson before. Men who work hard all day and party hard all night. They're attractive enough, with that twinkle in their eyes and the permanent smirk on their lips. The scruff on the jaw only adds to the appeal, and on Iverson, it adds a lot. I usually stay away from men like him. But something about that contemplative look in the eye got to me. The lost glint that settled deep in his brown irises.

I want to dance on the wild side, and he looks like a good partner.

My skin tingles. Will I feel the rough tips peppering his jaw on my skin? Will I get beard burn? A shiver caresses down my spine. God, I hope so.

The moon doesn't add very much light to the path of the headlights, but Iverson slows and turns into a drive. Trees almost conceal the opening, but it's an actual road that disappears into darkness.

I lean forward and peer out the windshield.

"I can go back," he says in that delicious, rough voice of his.

"I'm not scared." I should be. I'm with a strange man in the middle of nowhere. But god, I need to live a little. One night. That's all I want. One night.

Please don't be a dud.

He gives me a sidelong look. Is he reading my mind?

"I know I should be," I admit. "You're not going to kill me, right?"

"No. You're not going to rob me?"

"How would I do that?" He's too big, and I'd be an idiot to run off into the wilderness in the dark. I'd become a mountain lion's breakfast.

"Wait until my pants are around my ankles, and then take my wallet and my truck?"

I snicker at the image. "I have a feeling that if your pants hit your ankles, I'll be too distracted." I lean over the console. "I feel like you have a really big...wallet."

He barks out a laugh, and my heart does a flip. The faint lines that wing out from his eyes match his laugh lines. This guy can do both brooding and funny. All the moody cowboys I've met stay that way when they're around me. I'm supposed to keep my mouth shut and do what they say. I'm supposed to stay quiet and wait at home for their next instructions.

The trees thin and a wide parking lot opens in front of us.

The hulking shadow of an old building towers over us. He swings the pickup around to point the way we came. Then he throws it in park. I'd love to see this view in the daylight. It's been so long.

I really should be scared. We're alone. Does anyone ever come out here? In school, my friends even stayed away from it. Usually, because I knew of even more private places to party. "Aren't there security cameras?"

"No." He chuckles. "Nothing worth vandalizing."

I recall that. It's an old empty mine. This guy clearly knows the lore, and he's probably brought enough women out here to know that he's not getting caught with his pants around his ankles. "What about explorers?"

"Not at night, Sunny."

The way he says my nickname sends warm tendrils twining around my heart. That organ and my brain are coming up with fantasy futures with this man. He's sweet, funny, and seems aware of how I'm feeling. I haven't known him for more than an hour, and I'm already picturing a fairy-tale ending.

I can't delude myself. I haven't even known him for an hour, and I'm romanticizing him. At the end of what I hope is at least one orgasm for me, he'll take me back to my car if he's not a murderer, and we'll go our separate ways. A casual fling. Easy peasy. I press a hand to my stomach.

He runs his calloused fingers over a lock of hair. "Nervous?"

"Is it a stereotype to say I don't usually do this?" I lick along my lower lip. "I've had hookups, but not like picking-a-stranger-up-at-the-bar hookups." My face grows hot. "Just stupid college stuff."

He's quiet for a moment. "Make me less of a stranger. What's your favorite color?"

"If I call myself Sunny, it has to be yellow. Yours?" Oddly enough, this is helping me feel less like I'm acting out of character. Going to Bootleg should've helped with that, but I never thought that, of all places, I'd pick up a guy there.

"Blue." He leans his head on the headrest. "Blue skies, blue water, blue jeans. I'm a simple man."

I smile. His tone hints that it's a bad thing, that he'd like to be complex, but I've met too many complicated men in my life, and it usually means I'm strung along because they can't figure themselves out.

I almost ask him what he does for a living, but I need him to be a stranger, or I might go looking for him after this. Men don't like flings tracking him down, right? I don't need more ties to Huckleberry Springs. I need freedom to make my own choices. Just like I did to land me in this pickup.

Yet I want to know more about him. "What's your favorite song?"

"'9 to 5'"

A laugh sputters out of me. "Dolly Parton?"

"Surprised?"

"I expected a Waylon or Johnny or even a Morgan or Luke."

The corner of his mouth tips up. "I know each singer you're referring to, but they don't beat Dolly. 'Jolene' is a close second."

"Happens to be one of my favorites. Don't ask me to pick a top song. It changes with my mood."

He adjusts his position to angle toward me. "Favorite food?"

"Steak."

"That's my girl. Same."

I did nothing, but pride explodes in my chest. God, I'm easy. "Favorite animal."

He snorts. "A horse. If I could have one sleep at the foot of my bed, I would."

"Why can I picture it?" We share a grin, but the moment passes and sudden shyness strikes me. Can I go through with this?

"Tell me one thing no one else knows," he says softly as if he sensed my shift.

His headlights automatically shut off and bathe us in shadows. We've been sitting for a few minutes.

One thing no one else knows. Some days, I feel like everyone knows everything about me. Or thought they did. Tonight was my night for anonymity. After tomorrow, that would change. And I'd taken my night and asked this man to give me a good time.

His question weighs heavily. Something no one else knows. "You first."

His face is shadowed, but he looks away. "I want more."

Surprise breaks down the anxiety his question created. "Really?"

"I'm thirty-eight. I have this pickup and not much else." He stares at the shadowed building. I put a hand on his arm. "I want something for myself," he says softly.

I can pretend for tonight that thing is me. "I know the feeling. People wouldn't think so, but I do." Since he was more vulnerable than I ever expected, I think about my answer. "I feel like I'm betraying myself."

He traces the back of his finger down my cheek. "How so?"

"I have a path that I'm expected to stay on, and I shouldn't complain. I've been very fortunate. I was born fortunate. But it's just...I thought I'd have more freedom as an adult." I don't want to get into specifics, so I keep it general. "There are people counting on me."

"Same, sunny day." He wraps his hand around the back of my neck and strokes his thumb along my bottom lip. "I'm not such a stranger now, am I?"

"No," I whisper. His leather-and-fresh-linen scent fills the cab. There's no overwhelming cologne smell with Iverson. He's nothing like the guys I've dated since I left home.

Then his lips are on mine, and I forget everything. He starts slow, and I relax even more, draping myself over the console to get closer to him, to get more. His lips are soft, but there's nothing but firm man under them.

He knows what he's doing. From building slow pressure to parting his lips until my mouth is open and he licks inside.

I meet his tongue with mine. The caramel flavor of the whiskey he was drinking hits my taste buds, and I groan. He sensually strokes against me. Little more than our mouths are touching, but he's consuming me. The hot tips of his fingers are on my skin. His taste is in me.

He pulls back ever so slowly. I open my eyes like I've been drugged.

"I want you to get into the back seat, Sunny. I'm going to devour every inch of you."

He digs in his pocket, and I think he's going to remove a condom, but it's his key fob.

He drops it into a cup holder. "You ever feel like you gotta get away from me, jump in the driver's seat and take off."

Touched, I stare at the fob. The silver on it picks up slivers of moonlight. "What about you?"

"I'll be just fine, Sunny. Don't ever worry about me."

He tells me that while he's concerned about how safe I feel?

I could fall hard for this guy.

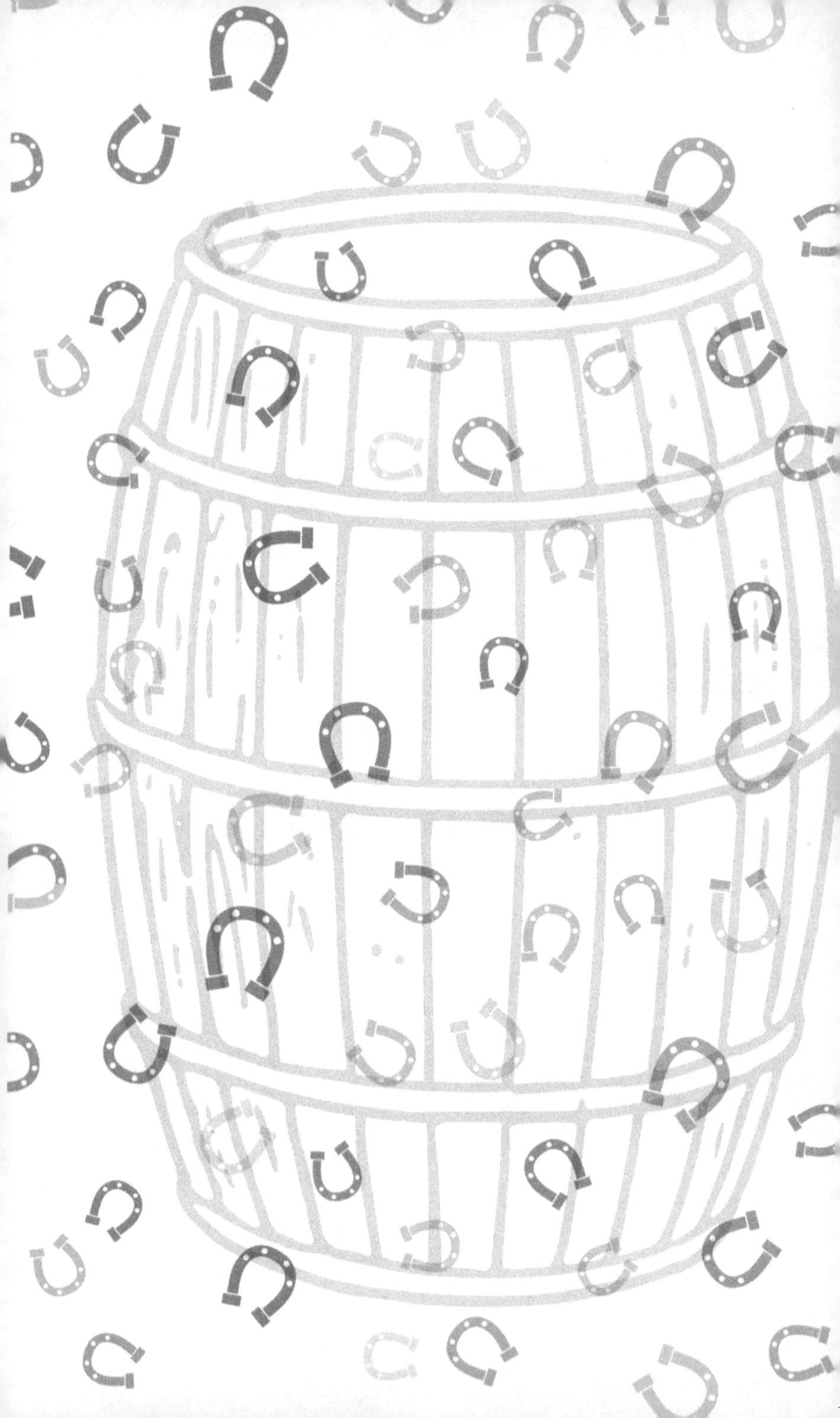

CHAPTER TWO

Iverson

She crawls onto the edge of the back seat, and I leave the door open. Half my blood supply is in my dick, and my heart beats against my zipper. I'm half afraid that once I release my erection, I'll come.

Once wouldn't be an issue. Mildly embarrassing, but I'm ready to go all fucking night long.

I put my hands on her bare knees. She tenses under me, but I'll take care of that.

The kiss in the front seat blew my damn mind. She's sweet and soft and smells just as summery as her name.

One of the straps of her dress falls off her shoulder. Her chest rises and falls. She's bathed in moonlight, but I'd love to see her like this in full sunlight. To see how brightly the coppery strands in her dark hair shine and how the amber flecks in her eyes sparkle. How creamy her satiny skin is.

I slide the other strap off her shoulder. The top of

her dress droops. She looks down, watching my fingers until I'm between her cleavage. Then, I slowly drag the top of her dress down.

I groan at the sight of her strapless bra covering perfect little mounds. "Your nipples are perfect little peaks poking through the fabric. Are they a pretty pink?" Tonight is shades of gray, but my brain happily fills in the details.

That delicious tongue of hers licks across her lower lip. "They're more like, um, reddish brown."

"Fucking perfect."

The clasp of the bra is in front. I could grin, but I am too intent on seeing as much of them as I can. Her bra falls away, and I drop it on the front seat. She sucks in a breath.

"You're not going to need that for a while."

Thanks to the dark, I can't see specifics, but the darker tips of her areolas strain out, pebbled and begging for my mouth. I dip my head and suck one into my mouth. As I skim my tongue across the peak, she buries her hands in my hair.

"Iverson." The way she moans my name is the biggest turn-on I've ever experienced. This whole woman is. She's vibrant, shy but bold, and so damn beautiful. She's a wildflower that got picked and has the audacity to still bloom.

I give her other nipple some attention. She arches her back into me.

While my mouth is on her, I slip off her sandals and drop them behind me. Then I push up the hem of her dress.

I kiss my way up her chest to the base of her neck. "I need to find out how wet you are."

Her eyes glitter in the dark, but she opens her thighs wider.

Fuck yes.

I pull her closer to the edge. Lust pounds through me, but I ignore my needs. She's my sole focus. I slip her underwear off and push her legs as wide as they'll go.

"I wish you could see yourself this way. Spread open and glistening. Your tits demanding attention."

Her chest rises and falls. The top of her dress is bunched under her breasts, and the bottom of her dress is gathered around her hips.

And that pussy of hers is mine. I hook my arms under her legs and tip her up until she leans back.

Then I feast. First, I lick through her seam. Salted honey lands on my tongue, and I know I'll never experience someone as sweet as her. Her tight little clit is hard and ready for me. I circle my tongue around it, and she trembles.

"Oh, god."

"You need to get off, don't you, baby?"

"Yes." She rolls her hips up.

I take a mental snapshot. Those dark eyes looking down at me from between those lush little mounds, her legs splayed over my arms, and a pussy that a man would ruin himself for.

I attack her clit. She's responsive, and getting her to the top of her peak is easy, but I back off, licking down to her entrance and shoving my tongue inside.

"Oh, god," she whimpers.

I tease her pussy with a finger. "You need to be filled, don't you?"

She nods. I push my digit inside to one knuckle and slide my finger in and out.

"Iverson."

She needs more. I give her one more knuckle.

She squirms, trying to sink into more of me, but she can't go farther than my shoulders will allow.

"Not yet, sunshine. I'm playing."

"You're being mean." But her lips are parted, her eyes are glazed, and she's undulating her hips.

I can do this all night. My dick is trapped, but this isn't retribution for making me wait. I'll wait forever. This is a treat I'll never have again. If I thought I wanted more before tasting her, I know I'll be yearning for this for the rest of my life.

I rise to take a nipple into my mouth. I play with the bud with my tongue while thrusting my finger in and out of her. A frustrated gasp leaves her, but she desperately rides my hand. Her walls clench around me, and her breathing quickens.

I abandon her nipple. "Not so fast, sunshine. I'm not done with my meal."

I withdraw my finger until she gets one knuckle and suck her clit into my mouth.

"Yes!" She tries to ride my face, but I clamp onto her thigh with my free arm. Her other foot is propped on the doorframe, and she's straining against it.

Greedy woman.

I put more pressure on her clit and thrust my whole finger inside. She's wet and dripping and ready to come. I stand, keeping hold of her leg.

"You are an infuriating man." She's breathless and on the edge.

I grin and take my wallet out. "You're suffocating my finger, sunny day, and I wanna feel that on my dick." I bend enough to lick across a nipple. "I bet you're so tight I'll hardly be able to move."

I rip down my zipper, wincing at the pleasure-pain zinging across my erection. I shove fabric out of the way, and my cock bobs free. My mouth pulls tight. Need pounds at my temples and desire pushes outward. The pressure's close to releasing.

One-handed, I grab onto the condom with my teeth. I yank the rubber free and toss the wrapper into the front seat. It'll keep her bra company. I have more condoms in the console.

The whole time, her gaze is stroking from my face to my erection. She watches me roll the condom on, and she bites her goddamn lip. "You're big everywhere."

This woman is going to destroy me.

I bend enough to tongue through her folds until she's squirming. So damn needy. Then, I rise enough to notch myself at her entrance. Pressure stops me. Her shiny eyes are on mine, and she wraps her arms around my neck.

"Relax, baby, and let me in. I'll make it good, I promise." I claim her mouth for a hot kiss and wedge a hand between us to circle her nub. She goes molten, and I push inside an inch.

She moans, breaking the kiss. "You feel so good."

I push in farther. Sweat's starting to break out on my forehead. I want to pound away. She can take it, but I want it all to be good for her. I wasn't driving in and thrusting away like a madman.

She drops her head back. "Feels so good everywhere."

I keep pressure on her soaked clit until I'm fully

seated. Then I release her leg to wrap my arm around her back.

"You're so fucking wet and tight." Like she was made for me. My own personal dream to show me what I really want. A woman who can look at me like I'm somebody and not a grungy cowboy. A woman who'll listen to me when I spill my goddamn heart with no warning. And a woman who makes me want to beat my chest because of the way she responds to me.

She hugs herself tighter to me, kissing my chin and my cheek. I'm pounding into her, trying different strokes and different angles, until I find one that turns her to butter.

Her mouth drops open. "I can't—too strong."

"Come for me. Come all over me, Sunny. I want to see you fall apart."

She tenses everywhere, and I can barely move. I'm in a vise of her legs, and she's gripping my cock like a life-line. "Iverson. Oh my god." A quiver runs through her, and then she shakes against me. "Yes, yes, yes!"

I grit my teeth, waiting out her orgasm. We could come together, but she's perfectly pliable. She's boiling hot and soaking wet and all mine.

Big pulses grow weaker, running through her walls and rippling over me. She's coming down from the crest. That's when I press a hard kiss to her and lay her back. My cowboy hat gets crushed and falls to the floorboard, but fuck it. I continue to thrust. My climax is banging at the door, demanding to be released, but I need to take it all in. Unbound tits jiggling. She's holding on to the headrests of the front and back seats to keep from being pummeled across the back seat. I hold on to her legs, the force of my thrusts growing.

"So good," is all she can get out.

I'm not fit for thinking. My teeth are grinding together. She's pliant. Jelly.

I push her knees to her chest and hold on to them so she can't scoot up the seat as I slam against her.

I lean forward enough to slip the finger that was inside of her into her mouth. Her eyes darken, and she sucks the digit in.

"You're a good fucking girl." Then I pop my finger out and use it on her clit.

"Iverson, I'm way too sensitive—" A tremble runs through her body, and her eyes roll back in her head. "I can't come twice."

"You already are."

She's fisting around me again. If the only reason for all my empty hookups was to have the self-control to get this woman off twice while I sate myself on her body, then I'll take it. Every night alone was worth it to experience this.

Her walls convulse, and she arches. Her voice echoes through the cab of the pickup. It's the sight of those little round tits straining for the ceiling that undoes me.

I punch into her once, twice, and detonate.

My release shoots out of me, and I growl her name. "Goddammit, Sunny." My hips buck while the rest of me is rigid. The sounds of wet slapping fill the night.

Finally, I sag over her, catching myself with a hand on the edge of the seat. The smell of sex and Sunny fills the air. I wouldn't mind if the pickup smelled like this forever.

Except one night is all I get. Then Sunny will go her way, and I'll go mine. I'll remember her each and every night I go to bed alone. And I'll wish she was with me, confessing something no one else knew about her.

Sunny

I've never had so much sex in one night. "I can't believe I'm going to come again."

The man got me into all sorts of contortions. I'd been belly down on the seat while he pounded into me from behind. I'd had my ass practically out the window while going down on him. He wouldn't let me suck him all the way off. *I've gotta come inside you.* He acted like a man obsessed. The experience was heady. He is also getting me way out of my comfort zone. I didn't think I had kinks, but this position suggests I have one.

I sit on his lap, with my back to his chest. My dress is in the front seat with my underwear and all of his clothing. Our shoes are in the dirt outside. He's inside me and gripping my hips. He's angled the rearview mirror enough that we can see where we are connected. My pussy is clamped around his cock, and I am rubbing myself off.

I won't be able to feel my clit for a month after tonight. But it's worth it. A night of backseat sex has shown me how boring my life has gotten. I don't know how I'd change it unless I could bottle Iverson and carry him with me.

But when we go our own ways at the end of the night —this morning?—I'll go home. I'll return to who I was before I parked outside of Bootleg Tavern. I'll be a good girl, but in a different way than how Iverson meant it.

"That's it," he growls into my ear, watching the same mirror show.

A drop of my wetness runs from my fingers down to where he is sliding in and out of me. My legs are wedged against the back of the front seats, and his powerful thighs are underneath mine, the muscles scattered with dark hair that scrapes against my skin and heightens every sensation.

I won't be able to walk tomorrow. It'll be hard not to wear a sign. *I got fucked all night long.*

He nibbles along the nape of my neck, and I shatter. My climax was building, but this guy can take me from five to infinity with his mouth and fingers. His big dick is a bonus. I've never been with such a complete package.

"Yes, Iverson. Harder!" I brace myself with my free hand against the roof, and he lifts me up and down on his magnificent cock.

He always senses when I am coming down. In the tight space, he flips me to the side. My cheek presses against the back door as he angles my ass in the air. He maneuvers his big body over mine. I don't have time to mourn, no longer being filled with him before he's pushing back in.

"Hang on, Sunny."

And I do. I meet every thrust with a backward motion. He rides me until he goes rigid. I've started craving that moment—when he's wound up so tightly he can't move as his orgasm hits him. All because of me.

"Fuck, Sunny. Your ass. Fuck." He kneads my ass cheeks with strong palms. He likes my ass in the air.

Like the other times, he descends from his peak and pulls me closer to him. The two of us cuddle in the back seat. I love the sex, but it's these moments I'm going to miss.

Would it be possible to see him again?

No. I'm just starting a career that I'm not sure I'll stick with. It's not fair to a guy if I start something when I might move along.

I relax into his chest. He hangs half off the seat and lets me have the most stable purchase.

How is he single?

What if he's not?

Would I know?

"I've gotta get you back," he mumbles into my hair.

"I know." I don't want to go. The pickup cab has become my little haven.

His fingers dig into my hip. "Get dressed, or I'm going to bury my face between your thighs, and I'll be late for work."

I giggle. Iverson has made me feel more cherished in one night than any of my exes. Perhaps it's our chemistry, but somehow, I don't think so. If he's single, it's for a reason, and it might be self-imposed. Regardless, I don't need guy issues in this next phase of my life. I have one big guy issue, and I'm not sure how to work around that.

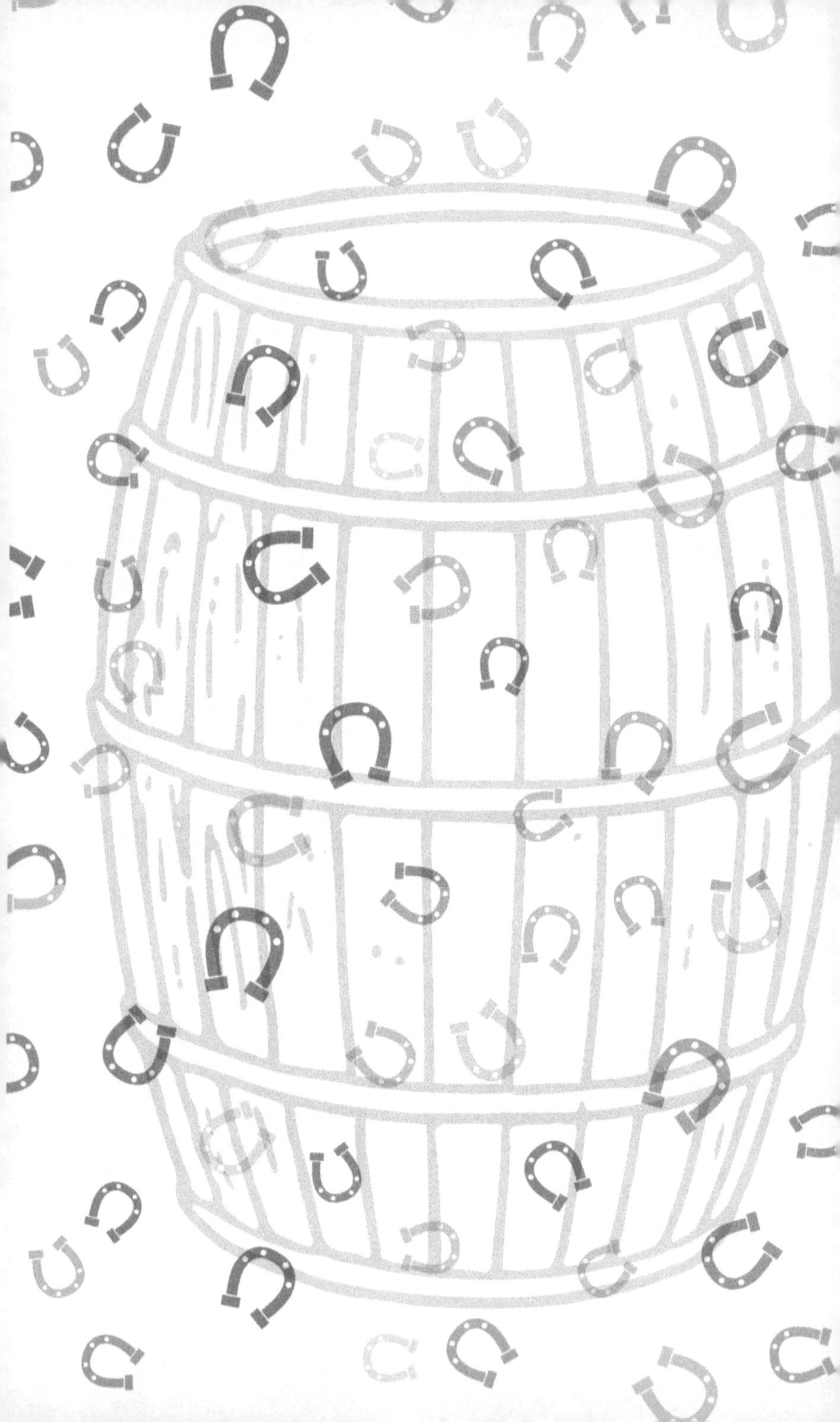

CHAPTER THREE

Iverson

I take Sunny back to her car and wait until she's out of the parking lot before I leave. It's a few hours before dawn when my ass will have to be in the saddle. I can catch a few winks.

Her taillights disappear down the highway. Is she really passing through and on her way to a different town and out of my life? Or will I run into her again at the grocery store? With fucking Andrew.

It's best if she leaves. I have a job that women don't like to compete with and a boss who doesn't understand work-life balance. Not that I need him to. The job has kept me and my brothers out of trouble, a spectacular one-night stand in the back of my pickup on my dad's property aside.

I scrub a hand down my face. All I wanted to do was curl up with her in the back seat and sleep until noon. Even better would be having her in my bed, but that's not possible. I sleep in the bunkhouse with my brothers and the three other guys who work with us. Haven and Durban would try to embarrass me around Sunny, but the others would try to steal her. Even the married ones.

I inhale the lingering scent of us in the cab and turn down a different road. I could follow her taillights, but that might creep her out. If she's staying at the motel on the edge of town, it'll still look like I was doing a drive-by. So I turn down a dirt road. It'll take me longer to get to the ranch and my bunk, but anyone still awake won't see my headlights rolling in a couple of hours before the day begins.

My eyelids are growing heavy when I finally park next to my brothers' pickups. Inside, I maneuver around the table and chairs in the kitchen area to the bathroom. We have actual rooms in the bunkhouse. William overhauled the layout ten years ago. He expects loyalty and dedication, but he doesn't think we should be living like we're at a youth camp.

I run through the shower, wishing I could save Sunny's sweet scent instead of washing it down the drain. Finally, I towel off and sneak into my bedroom. I get almost two hours of sleep before it's time to wake up.

My alarm is going off as I blink awake. I'm too old for this shit. My body's stiff in the best way, and if I think about why, I'll start the day with a monster erection.

There's a knock at my door a second before Haven leans in. His dark-brown hair is ruffled, and his jeans are undone with his green shirt hanging open over the waistband. "Late night?" he drawls.

"You wanna get dressed before you give me shit?"

He grins. "I am dressed." He leans against the door-frame. "How was your night?"

I scowl at him and sit up, swinging my legs down. "I had the meeting with Myles Foster."

He sobers. "He wants to buy Dad's land?"

Durban appears next to him. Unlike Haven, his hair is neatly combed even though it'll get crushed under a cowboy hat, and his navy blue shirt is tucked into his jeans. "Are you selling? Can we retire in the Caribbean?"

I laugh, but it's the first time Durban's mentioned not cowboying his entire life. "You want to retire?"

He shrugs, and it's not the immediate dismissal I expect. "Foster has the money to buy us a lot of freedom."

"It's family land," I say.

"We're not using it," Haven argues.

"You think I should sell? Just let Foster bulldoze over the memories we have there?" Myles explicitly said he'd be using as much of the old mine headquarters structure as possible, but I need to see how my brothers feel. We don't really talk about the property or what could be done. Any value that's ours is sunk into that land, but none of us have given a shit about money before.

Because we've never had it.

What if we did?

"We'll always have the memories," Haven says. He steps back to look up and down the hallway. Their rooms flanked mine, but it's morning, and the other guys will be moving around. "Be nice to have something of our own. We're not going to get that on these wages."

I drop my gaze to the floor. Did I make the wrong decision? Is it only me holding on to the memories?

No, I'm holding on to possibilities. "It just feels wrong to sell it off like it's nothing. The money split three ways won't last long."

Haven sighs. "That's true. Damn good fishing. Hate to give that up."

A tributary of the Stillwater River cuts right through our property. We know every inch of shoreline and have fed ourselves many times on the fish we caught. It's not like we couldn't go fishing anywhere else, but the spot we use for fly fishing is ours and ours alone.

"No competition." Durban props his arm on the doorframe. "He didn't make you an offer you couldn't refuse, and we trust you on that. The money's tempting, but these days, it goes fast. Still...did that conversation take until three in the morning?"

Definitely not talking, and not with Myles Foster. "Get out of here. Let me get ready."

My brothers grin at each other, then aim their shit-eating expressions toward me.

"Who was she?" Haven asks.

"Nobody." Acid burns up my throat on those words. They exchange another look. "Knock it off. It was nobody."

"You didn't go home with Tricia from the grocery store?" Durban asks.

Tricia's nice enough, and after a few years of randomly hooking up, she's been hinting about something deeper. I only slept with her because she was determined to stay single after a messy divorce. I've been keeping my distance since.

"Kaley?" Haven asks.

There aren't many eligible women in town who aren't

tourists or summer help, but we've each had our repeat partners. I haven't been with either Tricia or Kaley in months. They're both starting to want more. Kaley did find more with some attorney and cut me off. Whenever it doesn't work out, she comes back. I hope it does work for her because I can't give them more. If I had something to give, my brothers and I wouldn't be working some other guy's livestock, living in his facilities, or being told to keep our distance from the wealthy guests who can afford thousands for a week to feel like a cowboy.

"She was someone passing through." She said she might be, but as far as I'm concerned, she's gone. It's better that way, and the ache in my chest will get over it.

She's a Dolly fan too.

A few favorites and a secret confession doesn't make a foundation. Someone like Sunny should have more. She should have it all.

Both guys groan like they missed the winning lotto numbers.

Sunny's my jackpot, and I already spent it. My only plan for retirement is to stay mobile enough to ride until I die. The idea worked better when I was in my twenties and the morning stiffness wasn't getting to me.

Haven crosses his arms. "I had to sit here all night and listen to Cal clip his toenails while watching *America's Got Talent* because you were going to some boring meeting, but you were fucking all night long."

"I had the boring meeting," I mumble. "Then she showed up after."

"What's her name?" Durban asks.

"Why?"

He rolls his eyes. "Because I was on the other side of

Cal—and we all know he tries to use his teeth before he uses the clippers."

My empty stomach lurches. "Enough. I haven't had breakfast, and I'm going to lose it."

Neither brother moves.

"Name," Durban demands.

I wipe another hand down my face. They're obstinate enough to make us all late. "Sunny."

"Sunny what?" Haven asks.

"We didn't get that far. Now, move out of my way. William wants us there at nine sharp. We have a lot of work to get done first."

Durban snorts. "I don't understand why we have to go line up like obedient little servants whenever someone new starts."

"It's so we don't fuck with them." Our dad used to watch *Downton Abbey,* and Hawthorne Ranch reminds me of the show. There's a clear class divide, and the two can't mingle, according to William. But then he's the millionaire owner of a thriving working guest and vacation ranch. I'm just the help.

I wipe sweat off my brow and stuff my cowboy hat back on after a good dusting off as my brothers and I ride toward the main ranch. My brothers only looked at it and smirked.

Grasses rustle around the legs of the horses as we ride across the property. The working ranch around the bunkhouse has two large barns and a shop. Cattle pens surround the barns. It's where we keep the heifers when they're about to calve. The other cows are farther away but still close for when they give birth. The rolling pastures in the valleys of the foothills of the Beartooth Mountains are filled with cow-calf pairs. On the other side of the shop is the bull pasture. Next to them, the well-trained horses the guests use graze until they have to take on a new rider.

Three cabins line the property by the big house. The housekeeping and kitchen staff can live there or in town while the guests stay in the lodge.

The cowhands mill around outside the shop. Cal and the other two ranch hands are among them. I stop at the fence stretching between the shop and a bar and swing down. I tie off Burgundy, my mare, on a fence post, and she happily rips grass from around the base of the fence. My brothers do the same, and we join the crowd.

When William swaggers out of the shop, he pins me with a stern glare. "You're late."

I have two minutes to spare after having to make an appointment with the vet. The new VIP was less important than one of the cows under my care. "Sorry, boss."

He nods, his mouth in a satisfied line. He can talk a gruff game, and sometimes he's heavy-handed, but the most important thing is respect. As long as we show him respect, his tolerance is a lot higher.

William claps his hands together. "All right, everyone, thanks for coming."

He's dressed like us. Jeans, boots, and a cowboy hat. Only, like the guys who work with the guests, he wears a short-sleeved snap-up shirt. The rest of us wear ten-dollar T-shirts that are readily replaceable if they rip. Sometimes, when I get too much body fluids on myself, I just trash the whole thing. There's no coming back when a vet lances a large cyst and I get splattered.

I cross my arms and hang out at the back of the crowd. Haven and Durban are even farther behind me, less caring about who the new bookkeeper is. William's been cagey, which isn't like him. That's the only reason I was two minutes early instead of right on time. Curiosity is a big motivator.

"I know some of you have met Jamison before she left home," William starts. "She's been gone for a long time."

Haven catches my eye, frowning, a silent question in his gaze. I shake my head. I don't know a Jamison who's been at the ranch. I want to keep my job, so I only venture into the big house when William wants me in a meeting or needs hard data that only someone in the trenches knows.

William beckons toward the shop. "Jamison, the barn cats can wait. Come on out and meet everyone, hon."

Hon?

Shadows move inside the large open door, but I can't make out any details. I catch sight of a flowing skirt over cowboy boots. Her blouse is tucked in, and the sway of the skirt highlights the roll of her hips. Long, chestnut hair hangs over one shoulder.

My pulse kicks up, and I stand taller. Who is this Jamison? I crane my head to see her and every other man around me is doing the same.

When the sun hits her face, my lungs freeze. Pink lips that turn into perfect pillows when they're kiss-swollen. High cheekbones that flush during her orgasm. Amber eyes that match the shade of whiskey I was drinking last night.

Her gaze hits mine, and her eyes widen. Then those plump lips part.

"Sunny," I say under my breath.

Haven jerks his head toward me.

"Everyone," William says, "this is Hawthorne Ranch's new accountant. Jamison Hawthorne. My daughter."

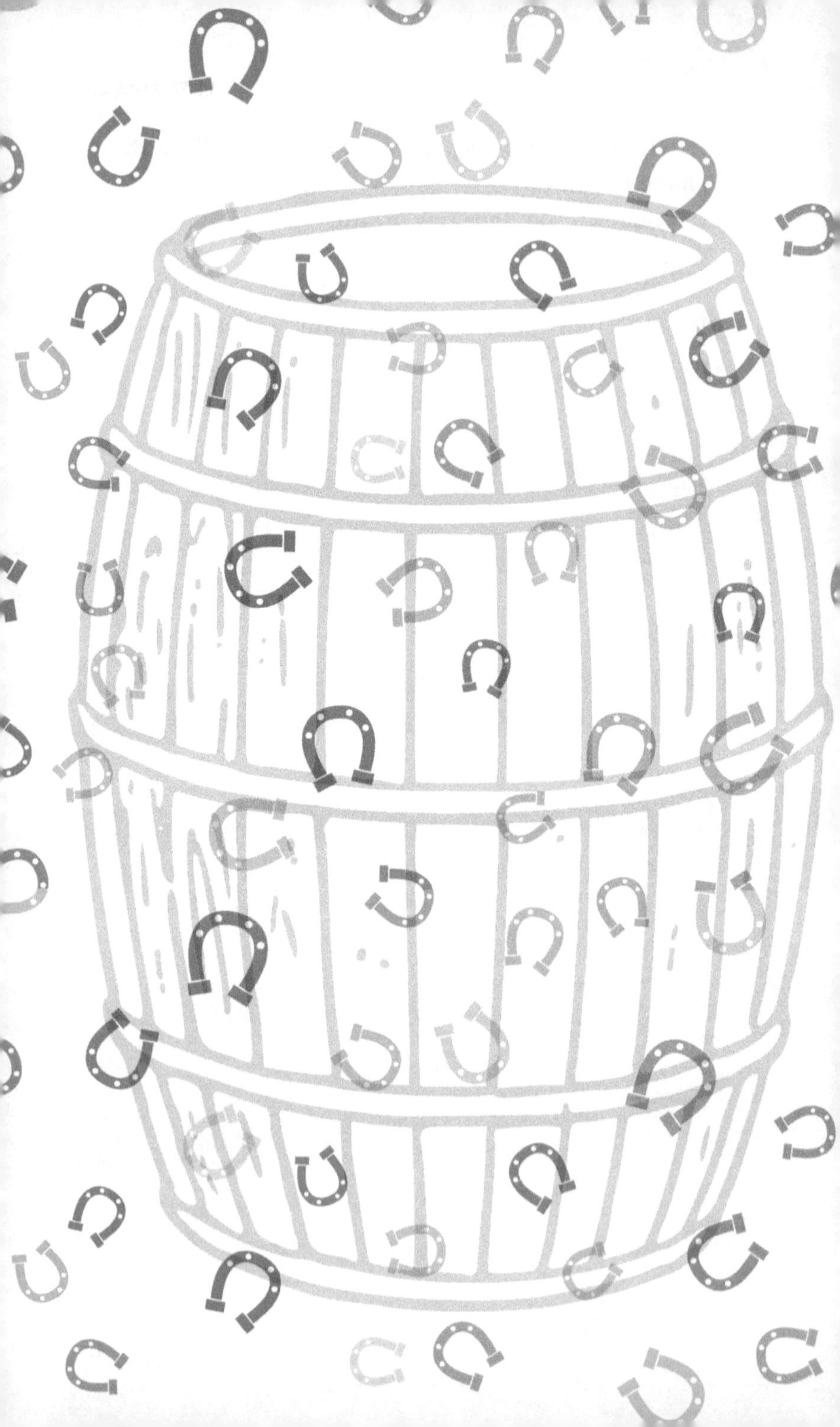

CHAPTER FOUR

Sunny

Oh no.

Oh yes.

Delight at realizing Iverson isn't completely out of my life dominates the emotions swirling in my stomach. Until his face pales and his expression begs for someone to put him out of his misery.

I don't have to ask why. Daddy is notorious for keeping his staff separate from the guests who pay exorbitant amounts of money to experience Montana ranch life. He's even worse about me and my little sisters.

I didn't grow up in the guest lodge, or the big house as we sometimes call it. Our home is closer to town and farthest away from anything to do with the guests or the employees. Daddy said he wanted us to have a normal life. We shouldn't grow up feeling entitled—we were—or to think we had everyone waiting on us—we did.

It wasn't until I went away for college that I saw how

good I had it. And how isolated I was. Walking into a job that was saved just for me doesn't feel as empowering as Daddy thinks it should. He says he raised us to be critical-thinking individuals. But he raised us to do what he wants us to do in life.

I give a shocked Iverson a hesitant smile, and his eyes only widen.

Hurt clenches in my stomach, but I force a bigger grin and meet everyone's eyes. They all look at me like I'm in a cage at the zoo.

Here, we have the endangered Jamison Hawthorne. She was raised in a crystal bubble, wanting for nothing and going horseback riding whenever she felt like it. When she was sent outside for chores, it was more like play because she, in fact, did not have to do chores every day of the week.

When young Jamison was sent to college, her daddy cut her off—sort of. Yet she knew that once she finished with her bachelor's degree and her master's, she had a job waiting for her.

Yes, look at Jamison Hawthorne. She walked right into a six-figure job while many of her classmates are trying to raise kids on poverty wages.

The hard part is—I do want this job. I love my home. I love Hawthorne Ranch and providing rustic experiences for others that I was lucky enough to be born with. But I don't want to be stuffed into a cage to do it.

"Hey, everyone." I wave, and my gaze travels back to those wide shoulders.

He isn't dressed much differently than when I met him at Bootleg last night, but damn, he looks good. Even better in broad daylight. Wide shoulders. Square jaw. Powerful stance.

The two guys next to him look from him to me.

One's brows are raised high enough to disappear under the brim of his hat. A shocked smile plays over the lips of the other. They both have dark hair sticking out from under their cowboy hats, with shoulders just as wide as Iverson's. Their stances resemble his.

Clarity washes through my veins, cooling me from the sun beating down on us. Iverson is one of the three brothers Daddy always talked about. He never said their names, just called them the three brothers, and he'd often reference the oldest as the supervisor.

Why did he have to be an employee of my dad's?

The crowd murmurs their greeting. Except for Iverson. His gaze is glued on me from under the brim of his hat, and his mouth is set in a hard line.

Quivers run through my belly.

Daddy's talking, and I struggle to pay attention. "So if you see her around, just know that she knows what she's talking about."

I smile. How strained does it look? Daddy makes it sound like I'm going to boss everyone around. He'd probably let me.

"Back to work," he says, and the crowd disperses.

People block me from Iverson, but when I catch sight of him, there's nothing but his back to see.

That's it, then. He's Team Daddy. He gave me an amazing night, but since I'm a Hawthorne, that's all we can have.

Maybe he's not interested in me.

The several rounds of sex in the pickup say otherwise.

Daddy's words growing up filter through my head. *Guys like that, Jamison, they commit to themselves. They work these jobs for the excitement and because, ultimately, the respon-*

sibility isn't there. The buck stops at me, not them. It gives them a freedom they can't get and that filters into their relationships. Men like these, Jamison. They're not good for you.

I don't know Iverson. But I want to.

Yet he mounts a gorgeous buckskin mare and rides away. It doesn't matter if Iverson is the best man in the world for me. A guy who can ride away from me like that either doesn't want me or doesn't want to risk his job for me. As much as I tell myself it doesn't matter and we only agreed on one night together, I'm left with an emptiness in my chest when he rides away.

Iverson

I have one brother on each side, staring at me.

"You're going to run your horses into Burgundy if you don't pay attention," I growl.

"Jamison Hawthorne," Durban says.

"What about her?" I know exactly what they're getting at. My slip-up saying her nickname will be one of my many regrets in life.

"*Jamison.*" Haven sucks his lips against his teeth. "Jami. Son. Jami. Son."

"Son." Durban takes over. "A lot like Sunny, isn't it, Haven?"

"I can see the connection," Haven replies.

I crane my head around. Is anyone listening to their bullshit? The others are taking a different path back, probably to check the fence like I told them to.

Durban rubs his chin. "I wonder if I ask Sunny if she had a late night last night, what she'd say."

"Don't you fucking dare," I snap. They would too. If I refuse to admit I know exactly what Jamison looks like naked in the dark, they'll find a way to get their answers.

"Jesus, Ivy. You fucked the boss's daughter?"

I grind my molars together. Yes. What happened last night was more than fucking. Was it the same for her?

Doesn't matter, jackass. Nothing's ever going to happen. Not as long as I want to work.

"She undressed you with her eyes." Haven rests his hands on the pommel of his saddle. We don't have to do much. The horses are used to crossing these pastures side by side, and they prefer going back to their familiar grass and water tank.

"She did not. I'm nothing but a hookup that I hope she never talks about."

"Most girls don't mention that to their dad." Durban makes a disgruntled noise. "We'd better hope she doesn't. Otherwise, William is going to cook all of us, not just you."

"Then you might have to beg Myles for an offer," Haven adds.

If my brothers and I get fired, it'll be all my fault. William can make our life hell. We all have heard stories about how strict he is when it comes to his daughters. Guys long before me were fired for hitting on them, smiling too brightly, and saying something suggestive. William Hawthorne does not play in business, and when it comes to his family, he's cutthroat.

Not many of the ranch hands were around before Jamison left for college. Her sisters are gone for school too, but the stories have been passed down. Mingling's not allowed in any way, shape, or form.

I indulged in my baser needs last night, and I've left myself and my brothers vulnerable. Myles Foster can boast all he wants about helping fellow fosters, but he's a smart enough businessman to know he holds all the cards.

I made us vulnerable.

The regret about Sunny isn't hitting as hard and deep as it should. I don't regret her. I regret what I can't have. If I thought I couldn't give her anything in the wee hours of the morning, I sure as hell have nothing for her now.

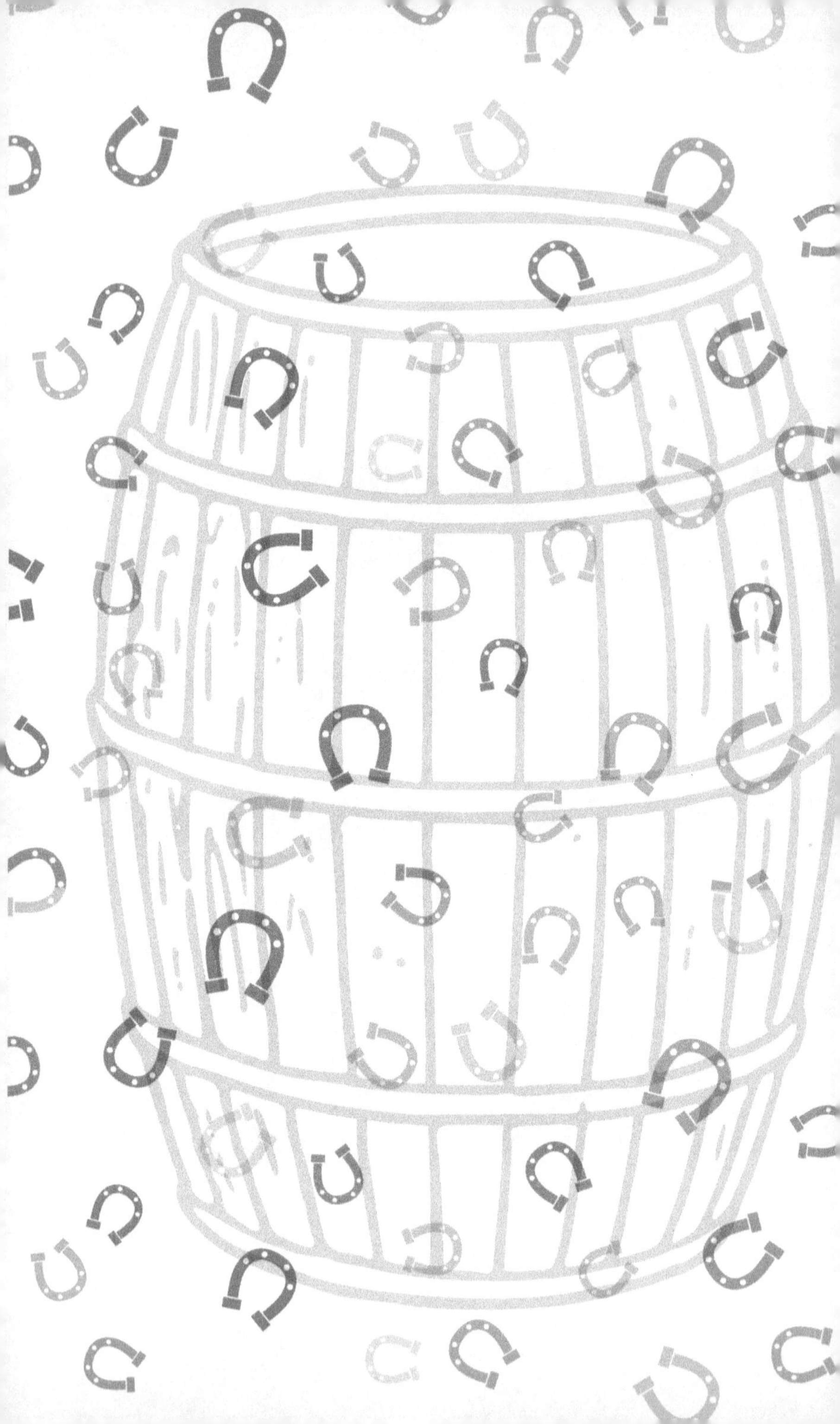

CHAPTER FIVE

Sunny

I just started my new job, and my boss is a giant headache. "Daddy—"

"We have weekly meetings. Sometimes, I'll call in Hennessy. It helps to have real-world insight into what's really used and how the money is spent. He does some of the ordering, but he's there for all the using, so I expect you to hear what he has to say. He's blunt. I'll give him that."

While my pulse spikes at Iverson's last name, I have to focus. "Daddy."

He continues pacing in front of the massive desk. The giant oak desk that'll be demolished with the house in a few centuries because it's too damn big and heavy to move is not what I want to work behind. Daddy had it built in this office when I was a kid. I have foggy memories of the assembly of the desk, the massive bookshelves, and then there're the custom paintings of the countryside—from an artist Daddy commissioned.

The office is ornately done in a very Old West masculine style. Not my style. Ideas to update and soften the look flow through my head.

"Every month, we meet with the county tourism board," Daddy continues. "They'll try to make it sound like they're helping us, but don't let them get high and mighty. It's this ranch that brings in the tourism."

And the rafting place, the fly fishers, trailer riders. Then there's skiers, hunters, and people who just want to get outside of the more expensive tourist traps in Montana. Daddy's talking like I don't know the area or how the ranch incorporates into the tourism. He's keeping a few things from me.

"Daddy, what happened to Glen?" The guy who occupied this office before me. Housekeepers and kitchen staff keep walking by, looking in, and once they see me, they tuck their heads down and scurry away. Is it because I'm the boss's daughter, or am I responsible for Glen's dismissal?

"He quit."

How did he quit? Why? I have to know before I can really settle into this office. "Did he get fired?"

Daddy frowns. "No, but he knew this position had a time limit. I was clear with him when he started that you'd be taking over when you were done with school."

That marginally makes me feel better. I'm thrilled to be home and have more responsibility on the ranch, but I don't want to start by creating drama with my mere presence.

Drama might be a little of what I need. "If he was good at his job, maybe he should still have it."

Daddy scoffs, puffing his white mustache up. "Glen started dating the head housekeeper. I think they were sneaking around behind my back because they knew he'd be free and clear soon."

"They're both adults." Both Glen and Inez were in their forties. Old enough to make their own decisions. "You didn't fire her, did you?"

"You know there's no fraternization."

Dammit. "Only nepotism."

Daddy's scowl deepens. "A drama-free business is a successful business. I can't have one section beefing with another because a date went bad."

He has a point. When I was younger, I overheard plenty of conversations between him and Mom about ranch hands and tour guides. Or ranch hands and house-keepers. Ranch hands and any other position at Hawthorne Guest Ranch.

None about ranch hands and his daughters. Only two people know about that. "You know me. Drama-free."

He shoots me a dubious look. "You have grown up a bit over the years."

I spread my hands apart and smile. When you cut a sheltered kid loose in the big, wide world, she gets into a little trouble. There's a popular sorority cocktail named after me. I'm not proud because it's called Sunny Side Up from the time I was caught skinny-dipping with the rest of my friends in the chancellor's pool. I designed the drink.

In fact, at most parties, I was the bartender. I took orders and cut students off. I even carded them. I might have gotten slapped with a fine, but I wasn't about to get in trouble for contributing to a minor or an accident.

I earned more respect from my unofficial bartending

than from anything else I've done in life, which isn't much. I barrel raced in high school, but when your parents sit on all the rodeo boards, it's hard not to wonder if it's me, the horse, or the money behind the Hawthorne name that's really good.

"I'll send Hennessy in. You should catch up, see how he communicates. It ain't for everyone."

Iverson's way of communicating is most certainly for me. "I'll be waiting."

Iverson

I take my hat off when I enter the big house and wipe the dust off the bottom of my boots. The employee entrance is through the side door by the garage. A hallway leads into the kitchen.

Cecil, the chef, tips his head at me, the dark skin around his eyes tightening when he sees my expression. "You aren't going to the pokey, are you?" He's joking, but he's not. I don't have a fancy culinary degree like him, but he's still felt the wrath of William Hawthorne when shit goes south.

"Depends. What's the new girl like?" I'm digging for as much dirt as I can without being suspicious. Any questions from me or any of the guys about Jamison Hawthorne would be noted and reported to the top.

The old accountant, Glen, was nice enough, but he never missed a chance to point out that his rank in the staff of Hawthorne Ranch was higher. Since Sunny is a Hawthorne, she's in the fucking clouds.

"I worked here before she went to college." He sidles to the edge of the bench he's chopping an onion on. "All the girls are a delight. I hope she's still as precocious as always." He winks and returns to his station.

She is. But I can't tell him that.

I walk down another hallway that's separate from the wing of the lodge where guests can lounge and visit. A small bar that I've never drank at is at the far end. Upstairs are all the guest rooms and an elevator is hidden behind the main-level bathrooms. The estate is sprawling. Sunny's grandma knew what she was doing when she built the big lodge and designed a vacation ranch around a working ranch.

William would lose his shit if he heard us make a distinction, but there is one. The working ranch is rougher, wilder, and we do things insurance won't allow with the guests. Cattle that are part of the guest ranch are kept in the most open pastures with the least amount of terrain change. There are no cattle drives through a creek wider than a yardstick for them.

My stomach fills with lead the closer I get to Sunny's office. I push a hand through my hair and dust off my front. A small cloud of dirt puffs off my shirt.

Shit.

William peeks his head out. "I seem to be waiting on you lately."

I came as soon as he texted. "Sorry, boss."

He nods, satisfied with my answer.

I follow him into the office. Sunny sits behind the giant damn desk. Only where it swallowed Glen, the monstrosity appears to bow at her boots. She wears another loose yellow sundress with her hair piled on top of her head.

Goddamn, she's beautiful.

I've never seen her before. We've never met. I don't know her. My dick needs to get that message pronto. I tip my head. "Ma'am."

Her golden eyes narrow. "Mr. Hennessy."

"Jamison needs to hear it like it is. Treat her like you would Glen." He claps my back and leans in. "But with a load more respect or else."

If he only knew I worshipped her body just last night. An uncomfortable pressure builds behind my zipper.

He leaves and clicks the door shut behind him. He never did like just anyone overhearing ranch business.

"Iverson." Her voice is a purr, caressing right to my cock.

"Jamison."

Disappointment makes her lower lip pout out. "You can call me Sunny."

"Beg your pardon, ma'am, but I can't."

A frustrated sound leaves her. "If you call me ma'am again, I'm going to tie your dick in knots."

I meet her gaze. *Promise?*

As if I said the word out loud, a flush creeps up her neck.

"You're blushing, sunny day. Is that what I missed in the dark?" My damn mouth. I came here to talk to the boss's daughter. Not flirt with my hookup from last night. She's supposed to be nothing but a searing-hot memory. "Fuck. Forget I said that."

"Why? It's true."

"Jesus, Sunny—Jamison."

Her sigh resonates loudly between us. "I didn't realize you worked for Daddy."

"I sure as hell didn't think you were a Hawthorne. What'd you mean that you were maybe passing through?"

She smooths a hand over her skirt. "I love this place, Iverson."

The way she says my name in the light of day, with all the familiarity of lovers, caresses my eardrums. I'd love nothing more than to hear it every day. But that isn't going to happen. She's off-limits as the moon.

"I love the ranch," she continues. "This job? I can't believe I can walk right into it. It doesn't feel right. But...I'm working for my dad." She taps her fingers on the edge of the desk. "What have you heard about me?"

She still hasn't answered my initial question, but I'll play along. "Not enough, or I wouldn't have touched you."

She points at me, her eyes narrowed. "Exactly." She rises and her dress swirls around her hips. I drink her in. She's not mine, but dammit, she's a sexy woman. "That's just it. My parents micromanaged us. Me and my sisters have all the freedom in the world, but we have none. I barrel raced in high school. Want to know why?" She doesn't wait for my response but throws a hand in the air. "Because I was told to. I went to school for accounting. Want to know why?"

It doesn't take a genius to see where she's going. "You were told to."

"Bingo! I got a master's degree in business administration. Do you think I was asked if I even wanted to?" Again, she doesn't wait for me but starts pacing in front of me, arms crossed in front of her chest. "This job was meant for me, and I want to be part of the family business. But I don't want to be in an ivory tower. I'm not going to live like I did when I was seventeen, getting told who I can talk to, who I can date, or what I get to do in my off time."

"He has his rules for a reason."

She gives me a flat stare. "You sound like a proper minion."

My patience bends toward breaking. She doesn't understand. She got the ivory tower. If I fuck up, I will be moving into that derelict mine. "Yeah, I'm a proper minion. My brothers work here too. We make our living here. It's not just me, sunny day." I wince at how easy it is to call her a pet name.

"Aren't your brothers adults?"

"Would you leave your sisters here if they had nowhere else to go if they lost their job?"

She blanches, but then she stiffens. "Actually, yes. They can handle themselves."

"Your sisters have resources. My brothers don't." The figure Myles quoted streams through my head. A fuckton of zeros follows that number.

"You have skills and a résumé that would get you hired on any dude ranch in the west."

This ranch is closest to my family's land. I didn't get long in Huckleberry Springs before we were taken away, but I'm here now. I don't want to leave.

I'm not going to abandon the last thing on earth left of my dad because I'm a horny idiot. "With all due respect, ma'am. I'm proud of my work. You might not have chosen to work at Hawthorne Ranch if given the option, but I did. So did each of my brothers. And I'm not fucking it up for some woman who climbed into my back seat."

Her mouth drops open with a gasp. Acid burns its

way up my throat. I was crass on purpose. It's necessary. Otherwise, I'll take her in my arms, apologize, and sweet-talk her until I get under that dress of hers.

Jamison Hawthorne is beautiful and sexy. She seems smart and driven and not just because of her family. She's loyal, and she indicated she's willing to burn a few bridges if she's not happy. She's the type of girl who makes me wonder what if...

"We're done here." Her voice shakes. "Some women have a job to do. You can go."

My boots won't move. I hurt her feelings, and I should leave, but I also can't keep coming back. I can't talk to her like I don't want to taste her again. "You can get information from any of the ranch hands for what you want. I'm not the only one with the knowledge you need."

She lifts her chin, her eyes sparking. "It's funny, Iverson. You told me in the dark of night that you wanted more."

I drop my gaze to the floor. "That's a low blow." I opened up to her, thinking I'd never see her again.

"I'm going to leave if Daddy tries to pin me into a life where I don't get a choice." She walks toward the picture window that overlooks the gazebo in the back-yard. Her arms are still hugged around her. "Why do I feel like you can have more whenever you want, but when the opportunity arises, you hide behind this ranch?"

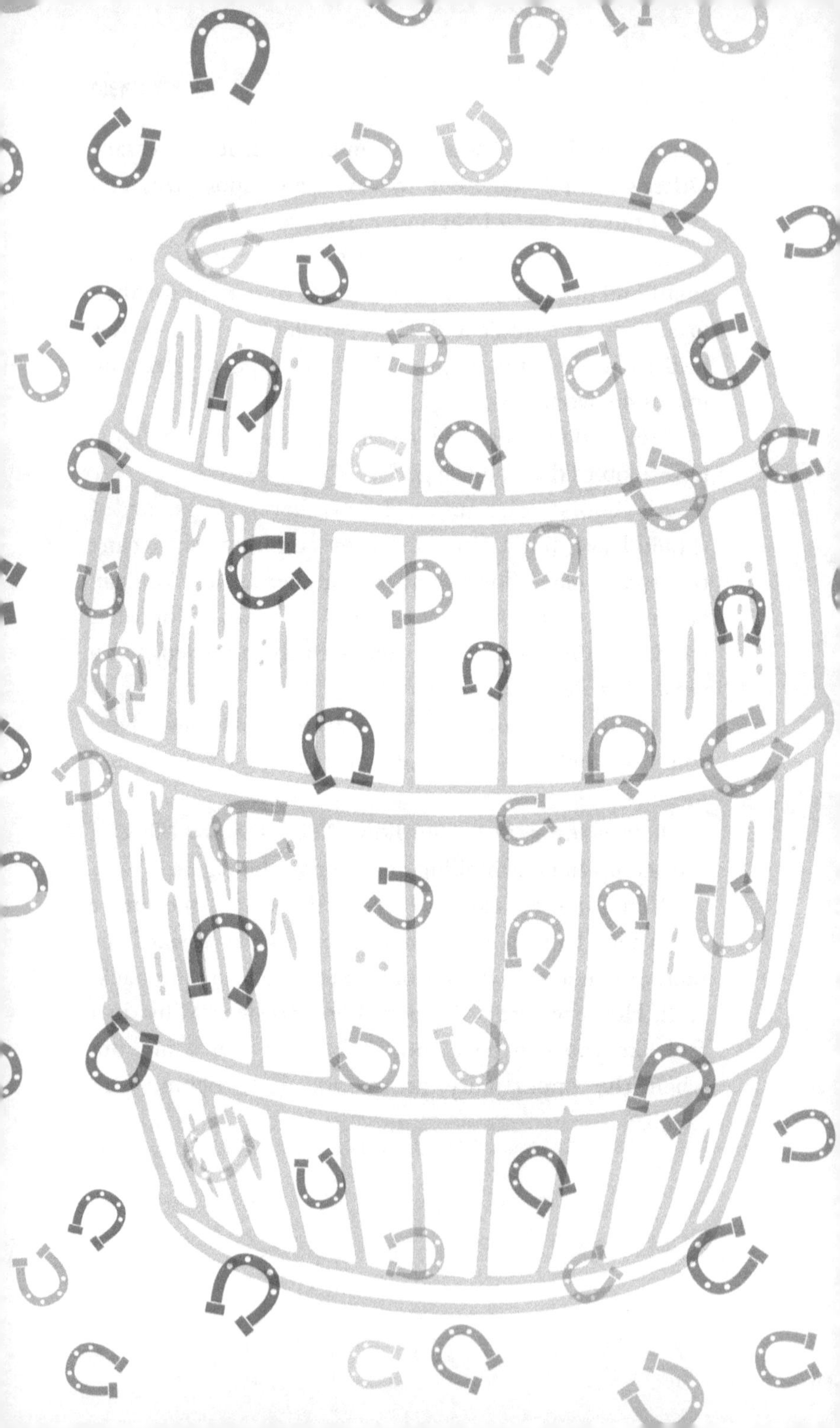

CHAPTER SIX

Sunny

I carry my morning coffee out to the deck of my parents' house. I've been staying with them for two weeks, but I need that to change.

My real estate agent sent me two listings. One's for an old house in downtown Huckleberry Springs. A small square house a block off Main Street. I peer at the screen and take a long drink of Chef's special blend. He added a ton of milk and topped it with cold foam, remembering just how I like it.

"Might need some work," I mutter as I read over the agent's insight. The house was old when I was a kid. The inside is cute enough, but do I want to be fighting old plumbing, a worn foundation, and aged electrical wiring?

On to the next listing. More than an old box with peeling paint, the second house is a manufactured home on five acres. It costs three times the amount of the first place. A broad deck sprawls across the front, but it's not enough to mask the blandness of the house.

No.

Ugh. I'd love to ask my parents' opinion and if they know of people looking to sell. But I can't. I contacted the agent two months ago, right before I graduated, and I swore her to secrecy.

Indignation warms my cheeks. I'm twenty-five. I shouldn't be scared of Daddy finding out I'm trying to buy a house. I am, though. He'd either coerce me to stay with him and Mom because it's financially reasonable, or he'd try to negotiate me into staying at the guest lodge. I know because he's already tried to bring up both.

What next? He finds me a suitable husband?

"Morning, peanut," Daddy says as he wanders onto the deck.

"Morning." I click out of the email and lay my phone on the table, screen down.

He takes a seat next to me and puts his old-fashioned Stanley thermos across from my phone. The thing is plumb full of coffee that he'll have finished by noon. "How's the job going?"

"It's good."

Two weeks of people giving me a wide berth and nervous smiles. I like it when I run into guests roaming the halls. They don't know me, and therefore, they don't avoid me. Instead, they smile and say things like, "Isn't it gorgeous here?"

To them, I'm either a guest or staff, and they don't care.

I'm staff, but word of how Daddy is when it comes to his girls has made its rounds. In case my little chat with Iverson didn't make that clear.

"You were quiet after Hennessy's visit," Daddy says gruffly. "Did he give you attitude? Say anything inappropriate?"

If only Iverson was deliciously inappropriate. The way he looked at me, struggling to remain aloof, while terror simmered in his brown eyes.

Between the time he dropped me off at my car and the moment I saw him standing in the crowd of employees, I built up the fantasy. He's a man who knows what he wants. He's a good man who'll take care of me and put me first, which means he'll stand up to Daddy.

Funny how I expect that of a stranger when I can barely do it myself.

I run my fingers along the back of my phone. I can be the princess locked in the tower, or I can be a damn adult who can face her father. "I'm looking for a place to buy in town."

Daddy's white mustache turns down with his frown. "You don't need to buy—"

"I want to. I'd like my own place." Where my parents stay out of my business. "I have an agent."

"I've got a guy you can use."

"I'm working with a woman." When he gives me a sharp look, I return it with a sweet smile. "She's good. I promise. I learned a few things from you."

"Hmph." His frown deepens. "Your mom and I like having you around."

"And I like being around you too." I really do love my family, but I need to set limits and maintain boundaries, or I'll always be the twenty-one-year-old college student who gets cut off, but not really. A facade of freedom. I want more. "I also like having my own life, and I can't do that under my parents' roof." He opens his mouth. "Or in the lodge."

He taps his fingers over his thermos. "This agent...is she finding you some good places?"

Surprised at his easy acquiescence, I nod. "As good as can be found in Huckleberry Springs."

His chuckle is dry. "You might be better off building."

Agreed. "I need to work a little longer before I can get the loan."

"There's ten acres close to town on the edge of our property you can build on. I can talk to the bank—"

"Daddy."

"—and you won't even need a loan. Your mother and I reserved some funds for you and your sisters for future homes—"

"Daddy. No." I push my coffee aside and lean across the table. "I'm going to figure it out myself." And I won't be building on family land. If Daddy's dirt is holding up my foundation, then he won't see a boundary. He'll think he has a say.

"Why reinvent the wheel? We weren't going to tell you until you were home for a while."

"It's not reinventing the wheel. It's boundaries. This is my life."

"You're my kid, and I provide for my family."

"You do," I say softly. "I've reaped the rewards, but I really do want to find my own home—whether I buy it or build it."

His mustache twitches, and he looks away. I can't tell if he is listening to me or biding his time.

I guess I'll find out soon enough. I take another sip of my coffee. "What's Hennessy's story?"

A crease forms between his brows. "Why?"

Because he can fuck all night and make me feel like the most precious treasure. Because there's something about him that draws me like a moth to a flame, and I don't care if my wings get singed. Because I've wanted to know everything about the man since I first laid eyes on him. "I figure since I'm working with him more than the others, I should have a good sense of him."

Daddy's hazel eyes glint. The perpetual protective dad. "His story isn't mine to tell. He's a good guy, but he's like any other hired man who's worked out here. A little wild. Doesn't let the weeds grow under his boots."

Really? It seemed like he let the roots anchor him to the ranch. "His brothers work here too? They're the three brothers you've talked about?"

"Haven and Durban. All good guys. Good workers and excellent cowboys. But guys all the same," he says with a warning tone.

I'm not going to get more out of Daddy, but I respect his stance to protect his employees. He might keep me and my sisters on a pedestal, but he does want to do right by the people who depend on him.

I grab my almost-empty coffee cup. "I'd better get to work."

"Have a good day, kiddo. I'll swing by for lunch."

Chef provides all the meals for guests and staff. One of the perks of working at Hawthorne Ranch, and it's a good one.

I'm grateful I have a day full of books to balance. It'll help me keep my mind off a certain Hennessy brother I have no business obsessing over.

Iverson

I'm in the tack room in the back of the barn with my brothers. We just returned from replacing a few hundred yards of fence around the winter pastures, and we're putting our gear away. Just like the barn that's almost nice enough for guests when the lodge is full, the tack room is fancier than any home I've lived in.

Wooden saddle racks line one wall in two rows. Hooks filled with lead ropes, headstalls, halters, and bits decorate the adjacent wall, and custom cabinetry runs along the top. Opposite the saddles is a bench with supplies for the vet when she comes. It's like a small clinic away from town.

"Did ya hear?" Haven asks, leaning against the bench. "Chef's making his honey-glazed pork chops with peach salsa tonight." He grabs his gut and moans. "Fuck me. I can't wait for dinner."

Haven has a bottomless pit for a stomach. "If the girls in town learn that they can get to you with food, you'll be buying a ring in no time."

"No girls in town are going to put up with our hours," Haven grumbles, then grins. "But they can feel free to win me over with a few meals."

Durban chuckles. "It'll be raining casseroles around here."

Haven moans again. "Don't mention food. Nothing makes me hungrier than fencing on a hot day."

My appetite has been gone for three weeks. Since I

found out the woman I can't forget is the most untouchable person on the planet.

To add to my shitty mood, yesterday, Myles Foster sent me another text with a higher amount for the old mine. As if his other offer wasn't generous, this one's high enough to make a guy pause. Am I doing the right thing holding on to that land? Would my dad come back from the other side and smack me for being an idiot? Foster's offer is life-changing money.

But how would our lives change? I need those answers before I make a decision. My brothers aren't aimless, but our options have been limited our entire lives. That land grounds us, while a windfall of cash would only attract the wrong attention. My brothers and I would be getting lured with a lot more than food if people found out.

Besides, none of us have Sunny's education. She can probably take that amount and grow it, while all I can do is monitor it as it decreases.

I haven't told Haven and Durban about the new offer yet. I will. Eventually.

"Think your girlfriend's still out riding?" Durban asks.

Awareness prickles over my skin. The last thing I needed to see today was her swaying gently on the back of one of the working ranch horses. She picked Mildred, a red mare with a sweet disposition and a love for pleasure rides. Try to get Mildred to work cattle, and she was as dense as a box of marbles. As a result, she was probably the best choice in the pasture when Sunny wanted to go for a ride.

The memory of seeing Sunny and Mildred on the far side of the pasture sticks with me. Her long hair must've been gathered under her straw cowboy hat, but she wore jeans. I'm practically salivating seeing her heart-shaped ass in jeans.

"Maybe," is all I say. "Time for chow."

Sunny breezes through the entrance of the tack room. "I hear it's going to be Chef's pork chops." She hefts her borrowed saddle onto an empty rack. She secures the straps and cinches properly, something I've had to get after some guys for.

"Yes, ma'am," Haven says, tipping his cowboy hat. "It's a big day when Chef makes his pork chops."

She smiles and puts the currycomb in a drawer. "It's been a long time since I've had them. I can't wait."

Haven and Durban flash me wide grins behind her back. I scowl at them, but my attention redirects right back to her.

She makes sure her saddle is balanced and nothing's crimped. That ass is better in jeans than I could've imagined. Round and tight. The topaz woven belt at her hips gives her an hourglass figure, and I remember every shadowed inch. Worse, I clearly recall how soft she is. She's got a T-shirt on that clings to her and amplifies the dip of her waist as well as her jeans.

Fuck me, she's a sexy woman.

When she turns, her gaze scans the room. "Where'd your brothers go?"

With a start, I glance around. Sunny and I are alone. Those fuckers. "They're hungry."

She tips her head. "And what about you?"

Fucking starving, but not for pork chops. My mouth waters like I'm ready to chomp into her. "I'm heading there." I don't move.

"Mm." She folds her arms, and the damn shirt pulls tight around her tits. "Me too."

I flick my gaze down her body and back up. She's watching me, but I can only be so strong. "Iverson."

I jolt. "Hennessy. Everyone here calls me Hennessy."

"There're three of you."

"They call me Ivy if there's more than one of us."

Her lush lips tip up. "That makes more sense."

What would it be like to have her under me with the sunlight on her? I would be able to see everything. Instead of dark shades, I'd get the prettiest pink of her pussy. The creaminess of her thighs. Does she have tan lines that I didn't notice that night?

Pressure builds behind my zipper. If I keep on this path, I won't dare go to dinner. I dart out of the door. "I've gotta meet the guys for dinner."

"Iverson."

I stop, tilting my head far enough to look over my shoulder. If I face her fully, my mind will dive right back into the gutter. "Yeah?"

"You really don't want to try, do you?" Disappointment fills her voice.

"It doesn't matter what I want. I respect your dad and my job." There's something that's bothered me since our last interaction. "About what I said in the office. I didn't mean to insult you. I'm trying to create distance between us." I need to.

Appreciation lights her eyes. "I know. Can't we at least be friends? We work together."

She's lying to herself if she thinks we're coworkers. She's part of my management team, whether she wants to admit it or not. "I can't be friends with you. Not when I know how fucking tight you grip me when you come."

Her lips part, and if I stay longer, I'll push her up against the bench my brother was just leaning on and peel those jeans off of her. And I think she'll let me. I walk out.

"Come to my office tomorrow," she calls behind me. "It's the end of the month, and I need to go over the next quarter with you."

"Can't." I keep walking. The open barn door looms in front of me. My escape from a woman who ties me in knots and makes me want to flip the table of my life. "Got fence to fix. You can ask Cal."

"Friday, then."

I continue right out the door without answering her. I'll be in her office because it's my job. And I'll look forward to it every day until then.

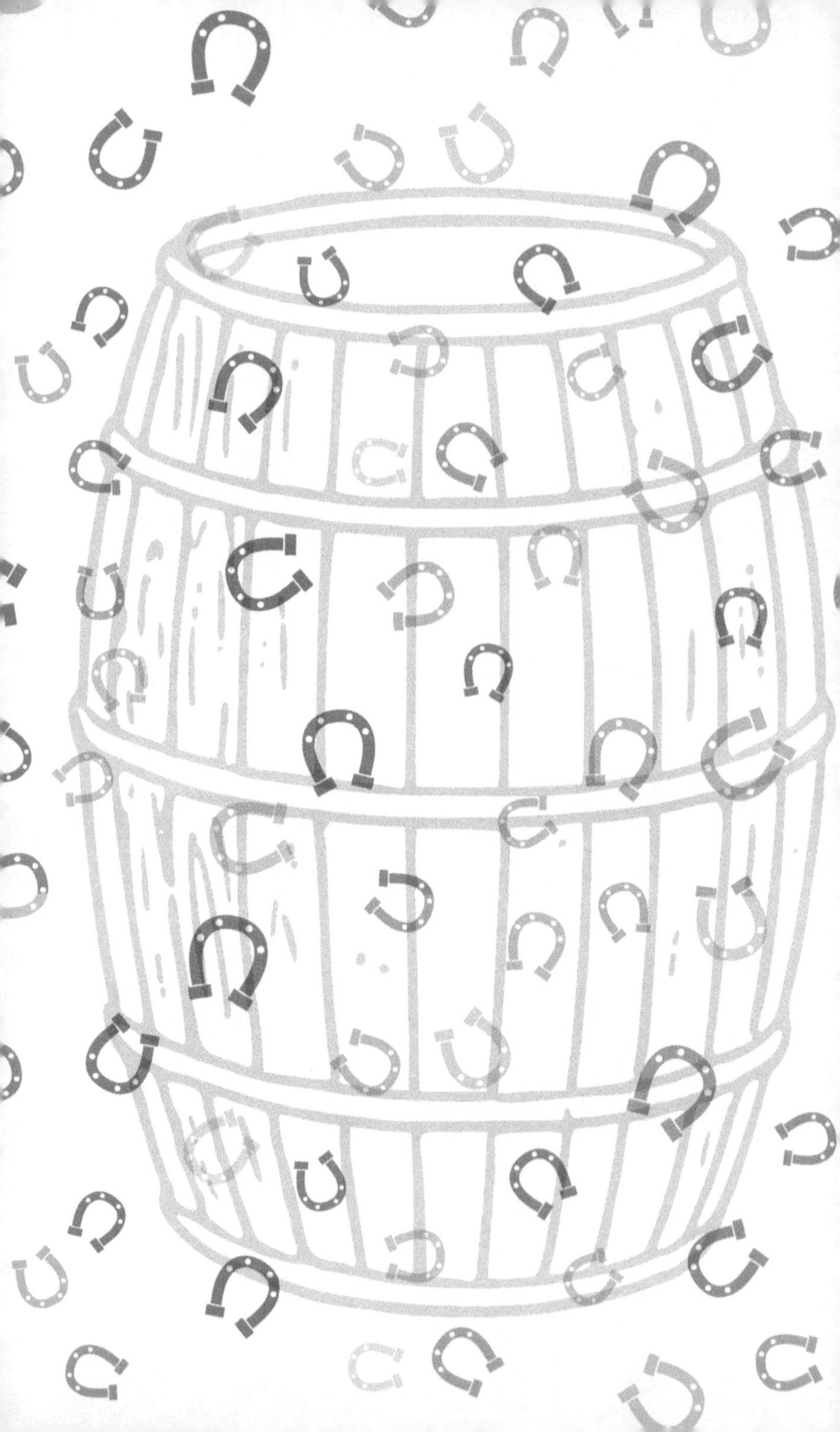

CHAPTER SEVEN

Iverson

I wait until Tuesday to go to Sunny's office. Each day has been torture. I have to be in the same room with her and talk about finances. I need to rattle off amounts and estimates of feed, hay, and repairs while my blood will be trying to vacate my brain and stream right for my dick.

Her door's open when I knock on it.

"Come in."

I enter. She's behind that massive desk. Her hair is piled on top of her head in a messy bun. My stomach sinks when I see she's in another sundress. A light-green one this time that gapes over her chest when she leans over.

She looks up from her computer and leans back in her chair, a sultry smile on her face. "I thought I'd have to track you down again."

"I do as I'm told, ma'am."

Her smile dips. "Ma'am again? I warned you."

I lift a shoulder and pull out my phone. I open my notes app and set it in front of her. "That's what we have for bales and how long I think they'll last. Thanks to the rain last spring, we have a nice supply, but I still recommend purchasing a few loads." I sit across from her desk. "Glen refused to try a new mineral because it's more expensive, but I have it listed for you to look at. Reviews say it's better for lactating cows, and I think it'd decrease our bottle calf rates."

"Okay." She scrolls through my down-and-dirty list. A furrow forms on her brow. "Self-propelled baler?"

"We do enough haying that I think it's justified." Her dad and Glen never thought it was. "It'd free up a tractor. Every year, we have to delay baling because we're still cutting or we have a breakdown. We can also change settings in real-time with the self-propelled option."

"You sound like a sales guy got to you."

I bristle. "And you sound like your dad. Maybe try haying one year and see how playing round-robin with the equipment bogs down your day."

"I sound like Dad for a reason." She keeps her defensiveness contained, but I hear it. "He's kept Hawthorne Ranch successful for decades."

I snort. "Yeah, and he's running it like he did in the past. Sometimes, I'm surprised we're not using horses instead of tractors."

Her expression stays serious. "Hiring another person and buying more horses is cheaper than a lot of this equipment."

She had me there, but cost wasn't everything. "Cowboys don't grow on trees, Sunny. Want to keep a good employee longer? Then make the job so their body doesn't give out so fast."

The squeaky wheels of housekeeping carts go by the door. Two young cleaners chatting about their weekend filters in.

Sunny goes to the door and closes it. I keep my gaze dutifully off her and the way her sundress drapes over her breasts to hug her waist. When she returns, she doesn't go behind her desk. She leans against it in front of me.

"How long do you want to be an employee?" Her voice is quiet, but her question seems genuine.

I grind my molars. I like the work I do, but getting up to toil all day for another man isn't the dream. Foster's offer runs through my head again. I have to talk to my brothers. We could do a lot with that money, maybe even start our own ranch. The irony that we'd have to sell our property and buy something smaller in order to do it isn't lost on me.

Is that what Haven and Durban want?

"As long as I need to be," I say, keeping my head down.

"I've seen Daddy's benefits. You can't work here for twenty years and have enough to retire. You're going to be working until you're almost seventy."

"Are you our financial adviser now?" I ask sarcastically.

"If you need one."

I blow out a hard breath. "I don't know, Sunny. Could me and the guys leave and do something else? Yes. But what? None of us have more than a high school diploma. Our only experience is what we do here. Sure, we've done some construction. We were on a road crew once. It's all back-breaking work. At least we enjoy this."

"I feel like you're underestimating yourself—and them."

"My brothers will follow me over a cliff." I clench my teeth. "It's a lot of responsibility."

"I can help with what you do have," she says softly. "I wasn't kidding about the financial advisor. I'm not one, but I understand it. If you trust me."

"It's not about trust." It should be, but I like to think I'm a good judge of character. My mama's responsible for that in all the worst ways.

I want to ask Sunny about coming into a windfall of money. Can she help with that? What would she do? I don't think she'd tell her dad, but I can't reveal the last offer to her before I do to my brothers. I can let them know we have someone who can help us do more than watch the amount drain slowly.

She's quiet, waiting for me to continue. I'm surprised I want to do just that. I don't entertain fantasies, and I don't share them with strangers. But she knows something about me no one else does. Might as well add to it.

"If the world spun in my favor," I finally say, "I'd like a ranch of my own. I'd call the shots. Hell, I'd love to ranch with Durban and Haven. As long as it has the name Hennessy." I run my thumb and forefinger along my lower lip. "I'd like to learn something new too."

"Like a hobby?"

I lift a shoulder. "Maybe. You know, there's this guy..." I clear my throat. I can't tell her all of it. Not without the approval from my siblings. "We go way back, and he started a distillery. Top-shelf shit. Real good stuff. The night you came in, I was pondering how he knew what to do. I knew he learned distilling, but it's the grains and the aging, and I dunno, the water?" I watched a bourbon documentary once in the bunkhouse. "It's interesting, but it can't be a hobby."

She tilts her head. "Why not?"

"Home distilling isn't allowed. I like beer, but not enough to make it."

Her chiming laugh is a treat to my ears. "I'm sure you'll find something, and your biggest strength is your family. Three heads are better than one."

I give her a long, lingering look. God, she's gorgeous. So out of my league, it's not funny. She didn't laugh at some poor cowboy telling her his hopes and dreams.

"Keep me in mind," she says. "I can help you with what you need."

I huff out a laugh and stand. "You are very much not allowed to help me with what I need."

She looks up at me through her long lashes. "And just what is that?"

"Another long night of fucking that sweet pussy of yours." I nearly choke on my words. Shit, where did that come from? How did we get so close?

Her face is inches from mine, and I'm towering over her.

"I need that too," she whispers, and it breaks the flimsy restraint I have. "I've thought of you every time I've made myself come since that night."

"You got yourself off thinking about me?" I'll never need help getting myself off again after that confession.

I hitch her farther onto the desk and sweep her skirt up. She works at the fly of my jeans, and as soon as her warm fingers touch the flesh of my cock, I'm toast. I'm hers.

"Sunny, I need to get inside of you now." I hook my fingers around the waistband of her flimsy underwear.

. . .

She's off the desk and pulling her skirt down. "Oh god, I'm sorry. I want you so much, but I don't want you to get into trouble."

My heart is pounding and my chest is heaving. Between how close to ecstasy I was and feeling like we were busted, my heart rate is sky-high. "It'd be worth it." I take her in, from her puffy lips to those legs that could've been wrapped around me, and I know one thing is for certain. She's worth the risk.

But I'm not. "It probably saved us. I don't have any condoms on me." I never replenished them. If it wasn't her, I wasn't interested.

"Oh." She blinks those big eyes. "Well, I'm on the pill, and I get checked yearly."

"I use the paltry healthcare we get here."

The corner of her mouth tips up. "I'm going to push for a better plan."

"That's my girl." I brush my hand down her flushed cheek. "I want you so bad."

"You can have me." She wraps her hand around my wrist, but she drops her gaze. "I don't want to get you in trouble though."

I cup her face. My decision is easy. I just hope I'm the only one paying for it. I've been a model employee, but I've never come across someone like Sunny. I don't want to waste whatever time she's willing to give me. "I never much liked being told what to do."

Sunny

. . .

I'm bent over the bench in the tack room. My jeans are around my knees. Iverson's hand is clamped on the back of my neck, and he's plunging into me. I bite my lip to keep quiet, but the ecstasy that swamps me is over-whelming. My teeth are going to cut through my flesh.

Worth it.

I reach the peak, and I want to hold it there. We don't have hours like we did our first and only night together.

"Iverson," I say his name on a breath. I'm begging. It's a plea to stretch it out. It's demanding he doesn't stop.

He slides in and out, an arm clamped around my middle with his rough fingers on my clit. He's got his other hand cupping a breast under my shirt.

"I've got you, sunny day." He backs off, holding me at the brink as his thrusts get faster and harder. "Now, baby. Come for me hard."

I grip the sides of the bench and grind back into him as I tumble over the edge. "*Iverson.*" Waves and waves of pleasure wash over me.

"Fuck, Sunny." His hold on me tightens. I can't move, and I don't want to.

There'll never be a time I don't want this. Him inside me. Filling me. I go to bed and wonder what it would be like to fall asleep in his arms. I know so little about him, yet I feel like I know more than most everyone in his life.

All too soon, he's pulling out of me and tucking that magnificent cock back into his pants. I tug up my jeans, wishing we didn't have to rush.

He spins me around and crushes his mouth against mine. We line up perfectly. My body's still thrumming from my orgasm, but his kiss is so staggeringly sweet I moan into him.

Eventually, he pulls away. "We can't keep doing this."

"I know." I dance my fingers over his collar. He's crowding me against the bench, and I like it. "I'm looking for my own place."

Surprise lights his eyes. "Bill's letting you move out?" He winces. "I don't call him Bill to his face."

I laugh. "You'd only do it once. Bill fits him a lot more than William, but he's all about status. As for your question, he doesn't have a choice." He only thinks he does.

Iverson feathers his fingers down my cheeks. The musky smell of sex lingers around us. "What's wrong?"

I must've been frowning. I hate to tell him about Daddy's plans, but talking to Iverson is way too easy. "He actually had it all planned out. He's saved money for me and my sisters, and he and Mom have decided where we'd live on the property. I think they even planned the houses they'd build for us." I squeeze my eyes shut. "Believe me. I know how insufferable that sounds. My parents want to build me a house. Poor me."

"It's controlling."

Thrilled that someone understands, I nod. "Right? He cares about us, but I'm trying to set limits." I rest my cheek against his hard chest. "Too bad there's nothing in town that I want to buy."

"Something will come along." He rubs my back. "We should get going."

"Yeah."

We continue holding each other.

Glad he didn't want to leave, I chance finding out more about him. "How long have you worked for the ranch?"

His exhale is long. "Five years. Before that, we dinged around Wyoming. My mom lived in Casper, and I stuck around until my brothers graduated. Mostly to make sure they graduated."

I tip my head back. "Wild childhood?"

"Neglected." The corner of his mouth pulses.

"Oh, god. I'm sorry."

"Not your fault. My dad's from here, actually." He rolls a shoulder. "I am too. But we had to live with Mom."

A few pieces click into place. "Hennessy. Like the Old Hennessy Mine?"

He nods. No wonder he knew the lot we were in that night didn't have security cameras. "Yeah, that's still ours. Dad made sure he locked it in our names. He did a lot of outdoorsy stuff and knew that shit happened. Only he had no one to ensure we went to if something happened to him. So we ended up with Mom when he was found dead."

"I'm sorry." I remember the story of a man going missing and his three kids being found living on their own. I only got snippets over the years, never any details, but I always wondered what happened to those kids. "I heard about you. Do you think we ever met as kids?"

"Honey, I'm a little older than you."

The way he says it sends shivers down my spine. His age is a turn-on. I'm sick of college guys with no life experience and the arrogant man-childs I seem to find who are my age. "Thirteen years is not that much."

"It is."

"You act like you're robbing the cradle. I've been to six years of college. Seven, really. I've worked part-time since I was faux cut-off and couldn't take huge credit loads."

His gaze strokes over my face. "I find your brain as sexy as the rest of you."

I'll take his compliment, but I hear the self-deprecation behind it. "You didn't go to college?"

"I didn't finish."

There it is again. The tinge of shame in his words. I hitch myself up onto the bench. My knees are on either side of him. "Circumstances, Iverson. That's the only difference between us." I drape my arms around his neck.

"I know William can be controlling, but he loves you, and your mom's not bat-shit crazy from what I hear. That's got to account for something."

"I love my mom. She's amazing, but I don't know." I run my teeth over my bottom lip. "She defers to Daddy so much, and I never liked that. I don't want a relationship like hers."

His eyes twinkle. "Something tells me that you won't put up with a relationship like that. You're taking a wait-and-see approach with the job."

I push my hands through his thick hair. "The first rule of any negotiation is that you should always be able to walk away. I'm trying not to get attached to being home so I don't convince myself to be meek and obedient." I'm doing a horrible job, getting attached to a handsome cowboy with firm roots in the area.

"What would happen if you left?"

"I'd probably get cut off for real." I smile. "Good

thing I have those shiny degrees I didn't have to pay for."

His chuckle is deep and pleasing. "You're always going to land on your feet, sunny day, but you don't have to leave to start over. I bet you could open up shop and get three customers right off the bat."

My heart cracks wide open. He's got so much confidence in me, and he's probably not joking about helping me, and he hardly knows me. I kiss him. "I could make sure those three customers know that they still have to do anything."

He grinds against me. "One of those customers wants to do you again."

Heat tingles over my skin, but we already risked taking too much time. Everyone's at dinner. I told Chef I'd be at my parents' house because I'd be out riding today. Iverson might be missed. "When can we do this again?" I hold my breath. Has he come to his senses? Is he going to tell me we can't?

"Where we went that first night."

The old mine. His land. It's been empty for years, and the area around isn't good for farming or ranching. He's too far southwest of town, and the terrain becomes too rugged. "What a beautiful piece of property to own."

"I go out there sometimes. Haven and Durban too. We hunt and fish." He drops his gaze. "Sometimes we just hang out."

"I bet there's been some good times there." I drag my hands through his hair again. He's opened up a lot, and I want more, more, more.

"Great times," he says quietly, his lips close to mine. "We talk about them. Try to hang onto every scrap of memory, and we do the skills he taught us. Makes us feel closer to him." Just when I want to wrap him in a giant bear hug, he places a kiss on my lips. A light signal that the heavy conversation is over. "But when you and I are there—I have plans."

"I already know how to fly fish."

He laughs and helps me down. "We'll have fun coming up with something new."

We make sure our clothing is straight. Time to leave our little sanctuary.

"I'll go out first," I say.

He yanks me to him for one more toe-curling kiss. "Saturday night. Eight?"

That'll give us hours and hours. "See you then."

Before I turn the doorknob, he says, "Hey, Sunny?"

"Yeah?"

"Wear a sundress."

I grin and yank open the door. At the opening on the far end of the barn, Daddy looks up. "There you are."

My heart stops. *Shit*. I could get Iverson fired just by being caught alone with him. I hit the light switch so he'll think I'm alone. The tack room goes dark.

"Daddy." I plaster a broad smile on my face and walk toward him. I don't pull the door shut behind me. It's usually kept open, and I can't be suspicious. "Have you eaten yet?"

"Chef said you were eating at home, but your mom said you weren't there. Thought I might catch you. Let's go look at the ten acres by the river, and I'll tell you what I'm thinking."

My hopes that he'll stay out of my business sink. "I'm working on it, Daddy."

He holds up both hands. "Just look with me. Hear me out."

If it'd get him off the ranch so he doesn't see Iverson sneak out of the tack room, I'll have to. "Sure. But don't get your heart set on me building on Hawthorne land. I'd like a place of my own."

"It would be your own."

No, Daddy. It wouldn't. Just like the man hiding from him isn't mine.

I'll keep working on both. Daddy's going to have to butt out, or else I'll move. And the connection I have with Iverson Hennessy is special, and I think we can have something real.

I'm falling hard for him. As long as he's willing to sneak around, I'm willing to hope we'll find a way to make things work for us.

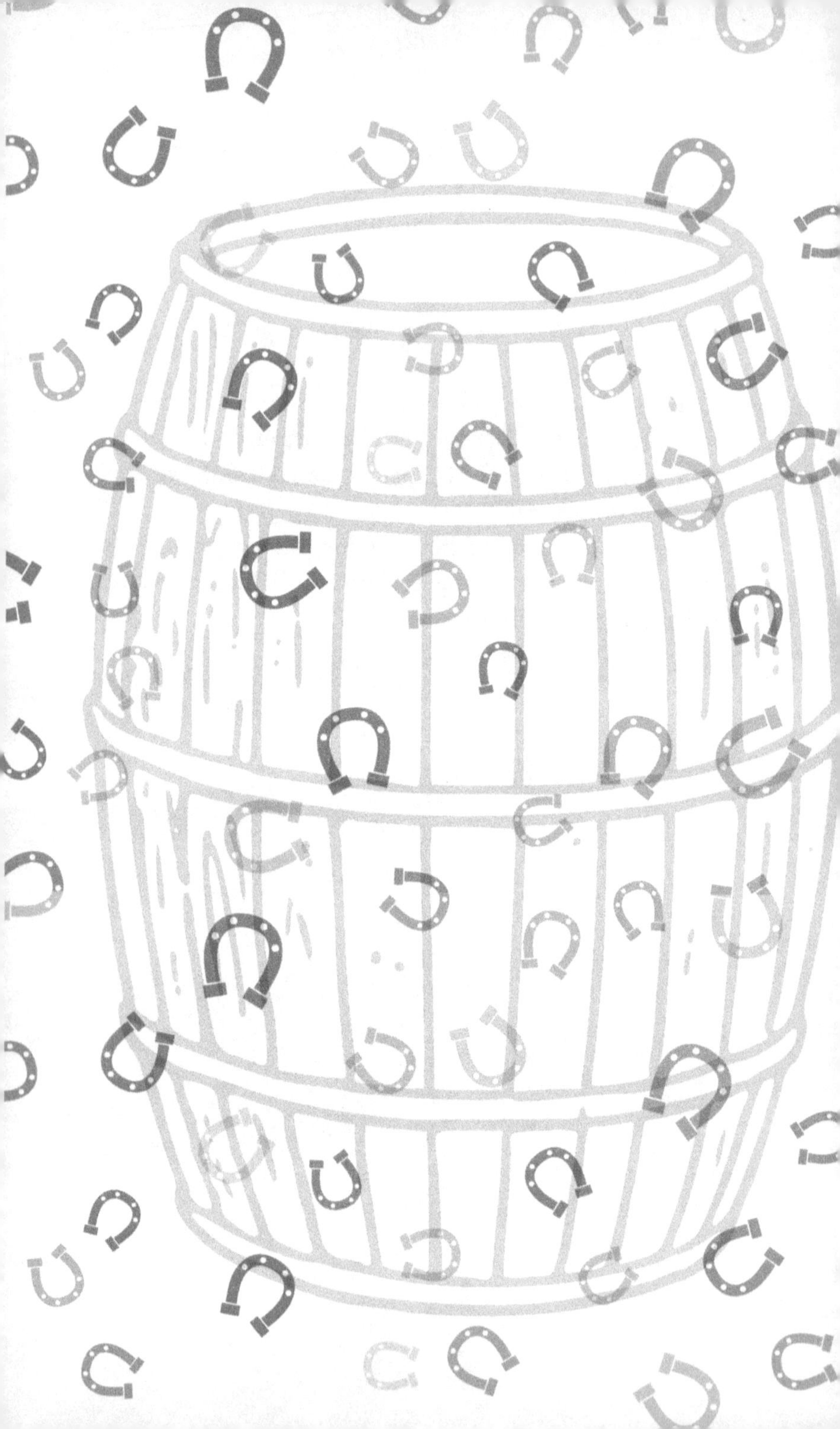

CHAPTER EIGHT

Iverson

I pull into the overgrown lot around the mine. Between me and my brothers, we drive enough to keep the main area cleared of weeds. Haven's pickup is sitting at the far edge. Hell. My brain is spinning for what to do. Do I keep secrets from them when I never have before? They won't talk about Jamison, but I'd rather clear it with her first.

Haven emerges from a trail that leads to the river. Durban's with him, and they each have a fishing pole resting on their shoulder.

Haven spots me and grins. "Hey. You missed the fishing."

Durban lifts the cooler he's carrying. "And the beer."

"You two taking off?"

"Nah," Haven says. "We have a few more beers. Thought we'd load our stuff and enjoy a drink to celebrate getting fuck all for fish."

Dammit. In ten minutes, Sunny would arrive. I skated on thin ice days ago, almost getting busted by her dad. Suddenly, I'm a teenager sneaking around all over town. "If I buy you both a six-pack, will you leave and have the beer at the ranch?"

"You know how prickly William gets when we drink on the property," Durban says. "He thinks we're all heathens looking for a reason to get wild and destroy shit."

Haven stops in his tracks. "Hold on. What kind of beer? Our choice?"

He'll get the expensive stuff. He likes trying craft beer, expensive spirits, and new wine. Even better if I'm footing the bill. But I have few other options to get them to leave. "Your choice."

Durban narrows his eyes. "Why?"

Tires crunch in the dirt behind me. I'm not the only early one. At least I don't have to think of a lie.

Haven's eyes light, and he lets out a whoop. "Ivy, you naughty boy."

"You're still fucking her?" Durban's brows are raised high.

"Don't talk about her like that."

His brows inch higher. "Like what? Are you *dating*?"

He sounds even more incredulous that there's more between me and Jamison. After my last two conversations with her, I only want more when it comes to us.

"No. Not dating." We're just fucking, like he said. Tonight's the closest we'll get to an actual date. Especially when I do idiotic things like buying wine and chocolate-covered strawberries for tonight.

Sunny creeps to a stop. Through her windshield, I can see her wide, questioning gaze. I wave for her to park next to me. She does and gets out. She's wearing the same yellow sundress from the night I met her. If that doesn't slap my dick awake, nothing will, but just thinking about Sunny is enough for that.

"We're busted," I explain as she approaches. "But the guys won't tell anyone."

Haven tips the ball cap he wears when he fishes. "Keeping secrets so our brother can get some."

Durban swats his arm. "Be respectful."

Haven grins, unrepentant. "Sorry, ma'am."

"Sunny is just fine," she says with a laugh.

Haven shakes his head. "No, ma'am. It is not."

"Jamison at least, please." She stops next to me. "Thank you for keeping this between us. I wish you didn't have to."

"Your daddy's right to be worried," Durban says, his expression serious. "Not all the men hired at the ranch are like Iverson."

She smiles up at me. "He is one of a kind."

Damn. The way she looks at and talks to me is the reason I can't stay away from her. The sex alone makes it impossible, but when I genuinely enjoy being with her, talking to her... I'm screwed.

My brothers study us. Haven almost looks disappointed, like he thinks I'm going to haul Sunny off and get married and to hell with the ranch.

The idea holds a lot of appeal.

Durban's forehead is furrowed as his gaze jumps between us. When his eyes meet mine, I see disappointment. I haven't told them I'm still messing around with Sunny.

That's not all I haven't mentioned, and I owe them a

talk. "Hey, uh, tomorrow we need to have a meeting. About this place."

Understanding fills their eyes.

"Gotcha," Haven says. He tips his hat again. "You two enjoy your night."

He and Durban hop in the pickup. Haven, the jackass, lays on the horn on his way down the drive.

Sunny watches them go. "I came too early."

I pull her closer. "I'll take you anytime," I say before I kiss her.

She smiles against my lips before she melts into my arms. Once we break apart, I murmur against her mouth, "I've been looking forward to this all week."

"Me too. I was worried it was going to rain."

"We can do just fine in the cab if we need to." But I'd rather be with her under the stars. I drop the tailgate of my pickup. "I, uh, have some wine and some snacks." My cheeks heat. Am I goddamn blushing?

Awe fills her face. "You have wine?"

"I couldn't find the Kinky stuff you asked for that night."

She grins. "I like wine. I like snacks too."

She's about to hop onto the tailgate, but I rest a hand on her hip. "I've got a pad and a blanket."

"You think of everything, Mr. Hennessy. Done this a time or two?"

She's kidding, but I'm serious. "No. I've never brought anyone here."

Her brows lift. "Never?"

"Never." She's special. If we have to sell this property, then I'll have one more cherished memory to go with it. My chest grows tight. I leave her to dig out the items I've brought.

I roll out the pad. I had cleaned the box before I left the ranch. Then I spread the blanket out. The day is warm, but nighttime might get a little cool. Next, I clip plastic dragonflies around the bed.

She taps a pink dragonfly. "Wanna tell me what these are for?"

"They're supposed to keep bugs away and don't stink like citronella."

"Interesting. I can't wait to put them to the test."

"I brought citronella just in case." I take her hand and help her into the back before I crawl in behind her. The sun is starting to sink behind the mountains in the distance. I have a few chemlights to crack for when it gets dark.

She digs through the grocery bag, pulling out the plastic cups I bought. "You really did think of every—" She gasps. "Chocolate-covered strawberries? Are these from Elodie's bakery in town?"

"Yes."

"She's not much older than me, and she was always making the best food in school." She opens the box and grins at me. "Can I have one?"

"Have them all if you want." I'm just enjoying her reaction to them.

She wiggles and plucks one out of the box. I'm in the middle of opening the wine with the corkscrew from the multi-tool I always have on me when I have to stop and watch her. Her plump lips wrap around the berry, and her eyelids flutter shut.

"Mmm." She takes a bite and chews. "Ohmigod. These are so good." She pins me with her gaze and juggles the cardboard container to grab a new one. "Here."

The berry hovers a few inches from my lips. Her fingertips overlap the flesh of the fruit. I take a big enough bite to lick along one of her fingers.

"Oh, Iverson Hennessy, you are a bad boy."

Her voice is a low purr, and her expression is provocative. I'm ready to ditch the drink and food and get to business.

Suddenly, it seems important to make sure she knows I'm not only here for sex. I could have sex if I wanted. I could be public about it. It's her I'm interested in.

I carefully set the wine aside. "I don't want to seem like I'm rushing you. I want to sit with you all night, but I need to see that body before all the light fades."

She places the strawberries by the wine. A sultry grin spreads across her face, and she yanks her dress over her head.

I'm greeted with smooth, bronzed skin. Her tits are cupped by a pale-yellow bra and her lacy underwear matches.

"Jesus, Sunny." I can't get enough of looking at her.

She pushes me back. "It's time for me to spoil you."

"Just having you here is enough—"

She yanks down my zipper and maneuvers between my legs. Her tits frame my dick once she frees it, and her ass is in the air. I can see it all with perfect clarity. "Fuck." *Thank you, sunlight.*

She licks me from base to tip, and I groan.

I prop myself on my elbows. "You're a goddamn tease."

She does it again. I twist my fingers in her hair, but I don't jerk her head around. She licks across the crown of my cock, and energy shoots down my shaft. Then she sucks me as far as she can into her mouth.

I nearly collapse back. The only thing supporting me is the need to watch her work my length, her cheeks hollowed and that ass within view. I roll my hips into her. Pleasure is building too fast and too hard as she pumps the base around my balls. When she opens her eyes to pin me with those amber depths, I have to drag her off me.

"Sorry, sunny day. I need to watch you ride me before it's dark." We have time. I just lack the patience. She does that to me.

She licks her swollen lips and grins. Pushing off my legs, she straightens and unhooks her bra. It falls free, and she drops it on her dress.

"Fuck yes." Her nipples are a perfect dusky pink. A little mole dots her chest underneath her right tit. I trace it with my finger.

The show she gives me when she wiggles out of her underwear is enough to get me off. I grit my teeth and savor the view, just like I'm going to cherish her later. By the time she straddles me, I'm shaking. And her groan when she sinks onto my length is lost in the night around us.

I grip her hips. "There's nothing like being inside you bareback."

"It's my favorite thing." She traces my lips. "One of them. They all seem to involve you."

For some reason, her words wind their way around my heart. We haven't done anything but fuck and talk, but maybe it doesn't need to be more complicated than that. "Tell me more of your favorite things. Like our first night together."

She slowly rides me. I can barely concentrate, but I force myself to.

She bites her lower lip and rolls her head back. "I love when you open up to me. When you hold me. And I can watch you ride a horse all day."

I roll my hips into her. "You been spying on me, darlin'?"

"Every chance I get."

I chuckle as I sit up enough to lick her tits and give her nipples some much-needed attention.

"Iverson." She's riding me faster.

"Take what you need." I slip a hand between us and find her swollen clit. "You're so fucking wet."

"I'm so close to—Iverson!" She arches and grinds into me, then shakes through her orgasm. She calls my name two more times, and damn, that's music to my ears.

Just as she melts onto me, I carefully turn her over and lift that ass back into the air. I plunge inside. It takes three thrusts before I'm coming. She's spread out beneath me, and I have my hands splayed on each butt cheek. If I could brand my handprints there, I would. I'll have to settle for having her like this as much as I can.

What if I could have more with her?

My climax slams through me. I grit my teeth and grunt through it. "Christ, Sunny."

I collapse behind her and pull her into me. She's naked, and I'm still fully clothed. I'll change that soon enough.

Sunny

. . .

"And then what?" I'm snuggled into Iverson's side. The chem lights leave the bed of the pickup in shadows. A faint scent of citronella surrounds us. The fake dragonflies add to the romantic ambiance. I flip the blanket over my bare legs just in case mosquitoes aren't dissuaded.

We're both dressed, and it's the middle of the night, but neither of us is ready to leave. I could fall asleep in his arms if I let myself.

Would I ever be able to experience that?

We can't do sleepovers. Renting a motel room isn't something we can do in a small town like Huckleberry Springs. People would know our business before we completed the registration.

"Then Haven went for a swim with his horse," he says. "It was the only way across the river."

Laughing, I snuggle closer. Tonight's Iverson is so much more relaxed than any other Iverson I'd met. He's not the brooding man I found at the bar. He's not the rigid employee trying to stay on his boss's good side. He's not vibrating with awareness, knowing in the back of his mind we could get caught.

This sneaking around is bullshit, but my job is secure. His isn't. So I'll get what I can of Iverson Hennessy and continue to want more. "I used to tell my sisters they couldn't go near the river during spring melt."

"Good advice."

"Daddy shouldn't have had you running cattle through there either."

"Better us than anyone else."

I lift my head. "Why?"

"We can do it."

I narrow my gaze on him and trace his jaw with a finger. "You're capable, but none of you are disposable."

He shrugs, but he hugs me tighter.

I turn onto my back and stare up at the stars. The moon is out and high in the sky. It'll be full in another week. In my periphery, the old mine looms, absorbing all the light. "Can you imagine how majestic this was in its heyday?"

"Can you imagine it as a distillery?"

That's an interesting idea. I sit up and picture what it looks like in the daylight. The large wooden structure is simple in its run-down beauty. "How much do you think could be saved to make it into something like Copper Summit? Have you ever been to Bourbon Canyon, where the headquarters are?" Copper Summit is the distillery heart of Montana. I haven't been there personally, but I've seen the pictures in the tourism guides. The place is gorgeous and had once been an old copper mine head-quarters.

"Once," he says curtly.

What's he not telling me? "Do you hate bourbon?"

"You know the family that runs Copper Summit?" When I shake my head, he sits up and props an arm on a bent knee. "My brothers and I were fostered with them."

"What?"

"After Dad went missing. Deep down, we knew he was gone, and we even..." His jaw turns to granite. "We even found him."

"Iverson." I lean into him, offering him as much support as I can.

His chuckle is dry. "I've never told anyone that. I don't think my brothers have either. He'd fallen down a steep embankment. The rocky trail we often used to hunt had given way. There was no way we could get to him or recover him. So we tried to live without him. But someone found out and reported us. I was only twelve."

I curl my arm through his. "Oh, Iverson. I'm sorry."

"Well-meaning church ladies didn't buy the story that our mom was on her way after a few months. I wish they knew what they were sending us to when we went to live with her."

I stroke his arm, sadness welling inside me for the lost boys who were terrified to leave everything they knew.

"The Baileys own Copper Summit. They took us in until Mom was located. We didn't foster with them for long. But they're good people."

"Is that where you got the distillery idea?"

He lets out a long exhale. "No. The guy behind Foster House whiskey was a foster there too. He wants to buy this place."

His heavy tone tells me enough about what he thinks about the idea. "You don't want to sell."

"This land is our home. It's the last place we were happy."

This guy is breaking my heart. I rest my cheek on his shoulder. "So you're not selling?"

"I haven't talked to the guys yet. We don't like the idea of being aimless millionaires. Like low-end millionaires. It's a lot of money, but shared between the three of us? I guess we could actually build a retirement fund so we're not in the saddle until we're seventy." He gazes at the mine. "But then this would be gone. Just like everything else."

"Maybe you could figure out some other arrangement."

"Like what?"

I lie back down and stare at the moon. "I don't know. Depends on what the Foster House guy is open to. You have the mine. He wants the mine. You don't need to sell the mine. The power is in your hands."

"He doesn't have to buy the mine. And he has the money. I'd say the power is not in my hands."

"You need to find out what he really wants. Another distillery? A piece of Montana? A connection with a fellow foster? Then you figure out what you want and pair them." I trail my fingers along his back. "I don't mean to be glib. It's not that easy of course. All I'm saying is that there's more than straight-out buying and selling. You have the property. That guy can get more money, but getting more land can be harder."

He yanks the blanket off and rolls on top of me. "I do believe I could listen to you talk about business all night."

I wrap my legs around him. "You know what else we could do all night?"

He rocks his hips into me, and the undeniable erection behind his fly hits all the right spots. "Let's see if I can guess."

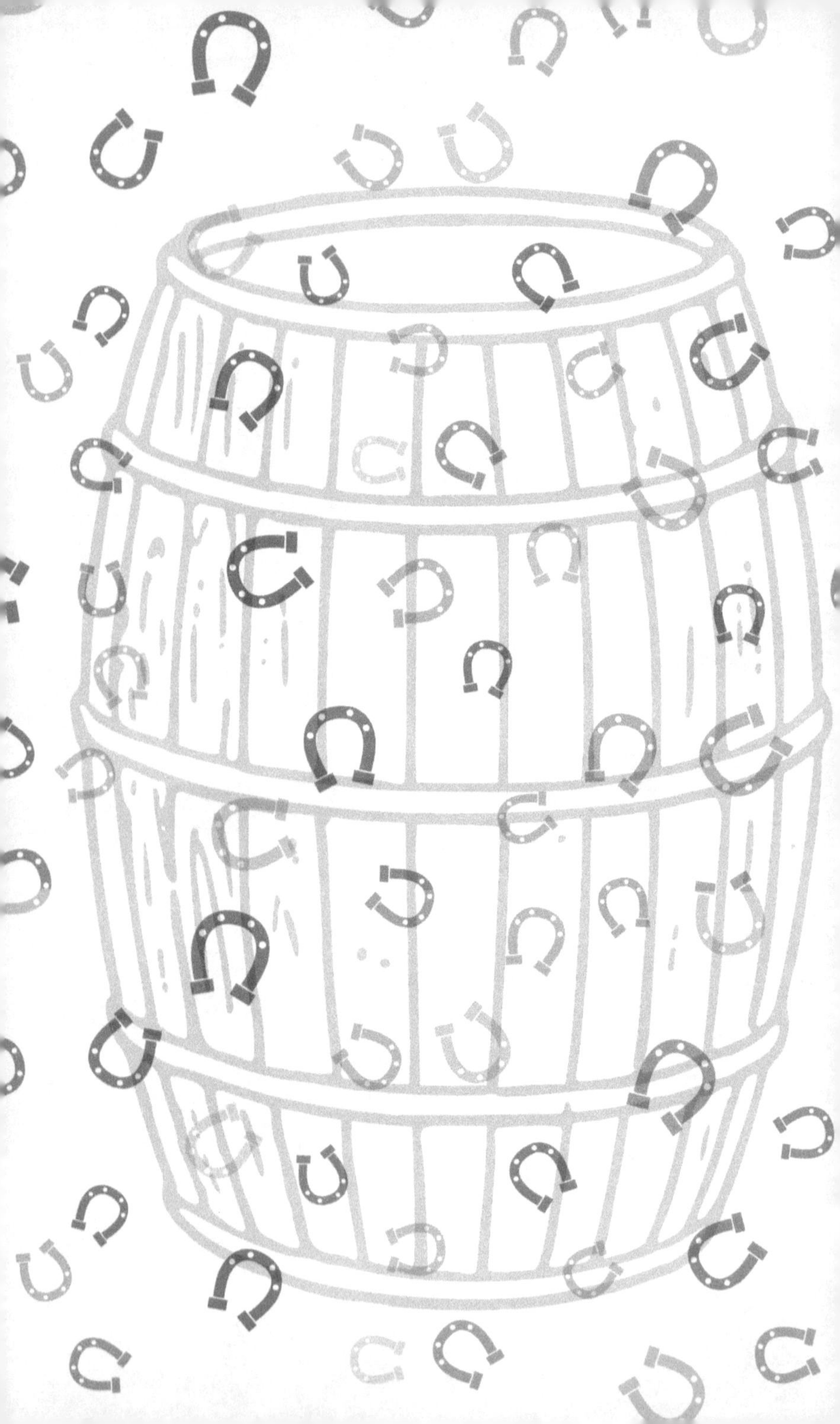

CHAPTER NINE

Iverson

It takes me a full week to catch up on sleep. I missed my brothers the morning after I got home from spending most of the night in the bed of my pickup with Sunny. They were gone fishing all weekend.

Since Saturday night, I've dragged ass, and they keep pestering me. But I've also been meeting Sunny in the tack room after her rides and going to her office for "meetings." The meeting usually ends with one or both of us coming.

I need to stop, but I can't.

Now, it's Friday, and I'm at Bootleg Tavern with the guys. I'd rather be with Sunny, but she's looking at houses with her real estate agent. She shot me a text with a picture of her and her dad. She was rolling her eyes, and he was looking out her car window and must not have seen her snap a shot. Somehow, he found out she was going and tagged along.

"Let me see that figure again," Haven says, licking the foam of his tap beer off his lip.

I pull the email up on my phone and slide it toward him. Durban waits on the other side. Haven whistles and pushes the phone back.

Durban peers at it. "Damn." He rubs his eyes. "It's real, isn't it?"

"It's a lot," I agree.

"Until you split it up." Durban taps the screen off. "Might have to push one of you off a horse."

"Haven's too full of shit," I say. "He'll bounce."

"I do bounce well." He takes another drink. "So. What are we going to do?"

"Sunny said something last weekend—"

"You talked to her first?" Haven's eyes are wide.

I shake my head. "Not about specifics." I tell them what she said.

Durban frowns. "What does that mean?"

"I dunno," I say. "I guess it's up to us to figure it out. Are we going to sell? Or can we come up with another plan? Do we want to come up with another plan?"

Haven pulls out his phone and starts tapping on it. "Speaking of figuring shit out—what about you and—"

"Not talking about that in public." I glance around. I already said her name, but not many people know her as Sunny. Everyone I work with refers to her as Miss Hawthorne or Jamison.

"Public." Durban snorts. "You two ain't exactly private."

Alarm trickles into my blood. "What do you mean?"

He shrugs. "It's probably because we know what you're up to, but you don't come to dinner like you used to. A routine that stopped as soon as a pretty little accountant started. Then there're the extra meetings."

"We're coming up with a plan to get us that baler." They both shoot me, *yeah, right* looks. "Is it that obvious?"

"I don't know," Durban says. "Once someone sees it, they won't be able to unsee it. Then what?"

"I don't know." I grind my molars together. I like being with Sunny. I look forward to seeing her. Holding her. Talking with her. "I like her."

"You're gone, man," Haven says. "Gone for her, but if William finds out, you're *gone*."

"We'll be right there with you." Durban sucks his lips against his teeth. "You both are putting all our jobs at risk."

"It's not her, okay?" I snap and look around. No one pays us attention, but Silas is a gossip. I have to keep my voice down. "I can't keep my hands off her."

"Right, and she's avoiding you to make sure nothing happens." Durban shakes his head.

"It's my fault. I've gotta cut it off." Pain flares in my chest, and I rub my sternum.

Haven groans. "He's got it bad." He leans over me to speak to Durban. "So what do we do?"

Durban flags Silas for another beer. The bartender nods from the other end of the bar.

I'm the only one drinking whiskey. Foster House. Will it be liquid inspiration?

"Between the three of us," Durban says, "we've got almost ten brain cells. Let's figure it out. You want to keep seeing Sunny, but William won't think you have a golden dick and wave his rules for you."

Haven nods. "He's got other daughters. He's going to

make an example of Ivy here to hold the standard for when all his little girls come home."

Haven's right. I'm not going to get special treatment. I never have. "You guys aren't making me feel better."

"We can find other jobs," Haven offers.

Not in Huckleberry Springs. "I'm going where you guys go."

"You're really going to choose us over some grade *A* —" At my glare, Durban's grin is rueful. "Gotcha. You like her more than you're letting on."

I scowl at my glass. I've barely had two sips from it. The stress of talking to my brothers and the fear that they'd want me to hold the course knotted up my gut. "She's young."

"She's young*er*." Haven downs the rest of his beer. "Shit. What are we going to do?"

"I don't know, but I have to decide." A dark cloud settles over my head. "I can't risk all of us being out of a job."

"That gives ol' Bill a lot of power over the three of us." Haven keeps his fingers wrapped around the handle of his empty mug, a thousand-yard stare on his face. "Can't say that sits right with me."

I agree, but I'm also not a dad. I don't have three girls to look out for and a thriving business that keeps a small town alive.

A knot forms in my chest. I might never be a dad. "She's his daughter."

Silas drops off Haven's beer. We all nod, pretending like we weren't talking about the juiciest gossip in Huckleberry Springs for who knew how long.

Silas gestures to my glass. "Got a new bottle of that."

"I'm going to drink enough to finish off the bottle

you've got." After this discussion, I have the urge to get shit-faced, but I'm old enough to know that's exactly when I shouldn't.

Silas waves a hand. "Nah, not that. It's the stuff I heard you talking to that city guy about." He turns and grabs a bottle with a familiar yellow label, only this one is lined with red. "Cinnamon. How'd you think they do that?"

"They infuse it with Ceylon," I rattle off, and everyone stares at me. I shrug. "What? It's what Foster said."

"Ceylon?" Haven asks, his interest perked. "What's that?"

"Not chemical flavoring is all I know," I answer.

Haven takes the bottle from Silas and studies it. "It's a darker brown. Almost cloudy." He hands it back. "I'll try a glass. Neat."

Silas is like our own personal performer as we watch him open the top and pour a finger into a tumbler.

Haven takes a sip and appreciation enters his eyes. "Gotta hand it to Foster. He knows what he's doing. I don't think I can ever drink the other stuff again." He passes the glass to me and Durban.

I taste-test it, letting the flavors roll over my tongue. The cinnamon is strong but pleasing, balancing well with the vanilla and oak notes. "Like candy," I say.

Durban nods. "Damn good stuff. Good choice, Silas."

Pleased, Silas limps away.

"Even if it makes Foster even richer," Durban adds when he's gone, then focuses on me. "Back to you, if you two get busted, what's she going to do? Let you get fired while she keeps her cozy office job?"

I don't know. "She chafes under his control."

"So do we. Yet we're good little boys," Durban says almost bitterly. "Seems like we're all stuck."

"Yeah. We are." I need the rest of that bottle Silas had taken with him if I'm going to go down this road. Maybe I should get shit-faced.

I let the last few weeks play through my head. My brothers are frustrated, but truth be told, we were getting restless before Sunny breezed into my life.

I study the squat glass of amber liquid in front of me. Then I look at the glass we've all taken a drink from and gushed over. Alcohol's never the answer, but whiskey just might be. It turned Myles Foster's life around.

"Hey, Iverson." The purr comes from my left. Kaley's on the other side of Haven. My occasional hookup. "Been a while. How've you been?"

"Busy," I answer neutrally.

"Don't look busy tonight." She rests her hand on her chin and stares straight at me like she doesn't see my brothers.

I only shrug. I've been doing enough of what I shouldn't be doing.

She tips her head, and her long blonde hair slips off her shoulder. "Why don't you come over later?"

The attorney and her must not have worked out. Both Haven and Durban tuck their chins down like they want no part of my answer.

Time to get the rumor mill going. "I'm hanging with my brothers tonight. Talk to you later?"

Her lips curve. "Yeah, we will," she says as she walks off.

That's not how I meant it.

"Are you going over there?" Haven whispers.

"You can have a real date," Durban says, but he doesn't sound happy about it.

"Kaley and I don't date."

"What a coincidence. Neither do you and Sunny." Durban's jab hits dead center of my chest.

"Jesus, Durban." I do a lot more with Sunny than I've ever done with Kaley or with any other woman. "No, I'm not going with Kaley." I scrub my face. When do I admit I'm lost for Sunny? When do I admit that I want more with her, but I have to be brave enough to drag my brothers along with whatever I decide?

"I don't like seeing you with your balls in a vise." Durban's expression is serious. "It's fine if it's balanced, but I don't know her. I'm worried for you."

Haven grunts. "Especially when our balls are in that vice with you."

I've always looked out for them. I'm the one who leads. It's always been that way, and they trust me. I hate feeling like I have to choose between my brothers and the woman I'm crazy about. They're not asking me to, but it's my job to make sure they don't have to.

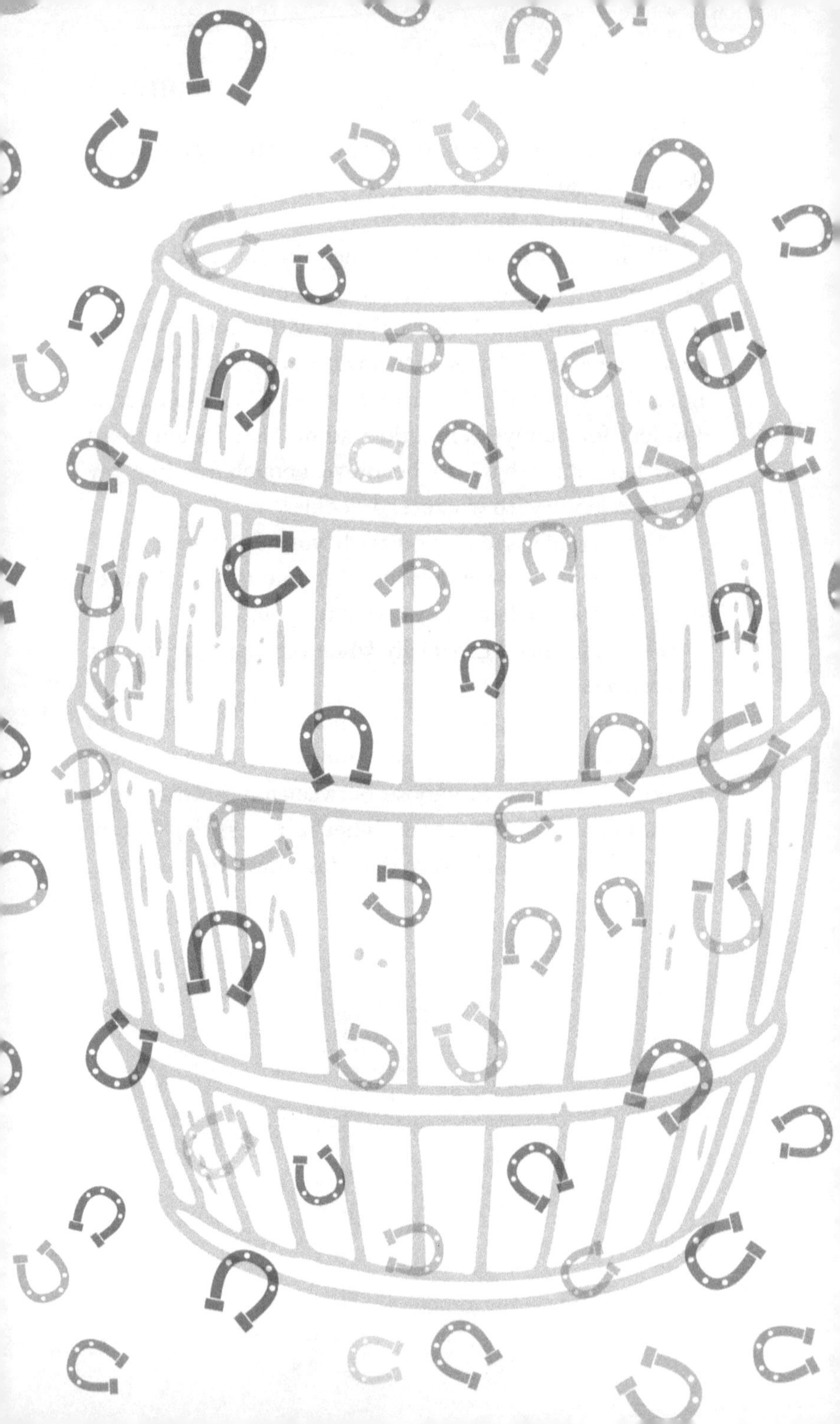

CHAPTER TEN

Sunny

I try not to look at the clock on the wall for the hundredth time. Iverson is due in the office in a few minutes. My stomach has been fluttering since this morning. We have to act like professionals. No quick fuck like the last time he was in my office.

I want a quick fuck. I'm addicted to that man.

After our second night at the mine, Iverson and I settled into a routine of meeting there a few times a week. On the weekends, his brothers are there. Iverson and I will just talk until they come back from the river and leave. It's safer than the tack room.

It's only been three weeks, but I worry that Iverson is going to put a stop to our clandestine meetings. He's been quiet. Still sweet and thoughtful, but something's keeping him in his head. Is he getting tired of sneaking around like I am?

He told me about that woman who propositioned

him at the bar and that he doesn't plan to take her up on it. He thought I should know in case I hear something and point out it's another change in his routine. People could talk, but he doesn't care. Then I won't care.

But also, how could that woman have had Iverson and then walked away? Her mistake is my good fortune. One day, it'll be my heartbreak. Waiting for someone to catch us grates on my nerves.

The sneaking around, it's wearing on me. The last time I left to spend a Saturday night in Iverson's arms under the shadow of the mine, Daddy pestered me about where I was going. He asked about friends I was seeing, who I was spending all my time with, and what we were doing.

I hated lying, but I told him I was stargazing and getting some me time. I was gone from home for years for school, and I wanted to reconnect with the land. He must not have believed me, so Mom started in. She wanted to come along, but I'd left before she could get ready. I got the silent treatment for a week.

It was easier to sneak out of the house when I was in high school. But then I had my sisters to help me lie and figure out a plan. They were usually crawling out windows with me. Even then, we didn't dare spend too much time at whatever house or pasture party we frequented. Our presence would rain hell down on the host if we were found out.

There's a knock on the door, and I look up. Iverson's got a sexy smile on his face, and he's leaning against the doorframe. He's got a hip cocked out and a thumb hooked in his pocket. His cowboy hat is in his other hand, resting against his thigh. "I can see that beautiful brain working, Sunny."

"It is." Always about him.

He glances down either side of the hallway before sauntering in, closing the door behind him.

I rise and circle around my desk. All the pent-up stress and desire since our last time together push at the seams of my mind, anticipating the release. "I've been waiting for you."

He closes the distance and tosses his hat on my desk, then curls an arm around my waist, drawing me in tight. "You're not the only one."

His lips meet mine, and the simmering heat in my stomach blooms. I wrap my arms around his neck and greedily kiss him back. It's Wednesday, and we haven't crossed paths since our Saturday night under the stars.

The door squeaks open, and I jump back with a gasp.

Iverson's arms reluctantly slip from around me, and a flash of disappointment hits his eyes. Guilt immediately wells inside me.

Daddy's glaring at us from the doorway. "I knew it," he grits out. He points a beefy finger toward Iverson. "Pack your shit and get out."

"Daddy—"

"Tell Durban and Haven that I'll send their last checks with yours." Daddy's face is red, and if Mom didn't have him on a strict blood pressure diet after some heart episodes years ago, I'd be worried.

"You'd fire my brothers because of me?" Iverson asks, as calm as I'd ever seen him, but then we all know the answer. Is he finally relieved to be done with the worry? To be done with me?

Daddy waggles his finger. "Do they know about this?"

"No," I say.

"Yes," Iverson speaks over me. "We're all adults."

"She's my daughter, and you were told the rules," Daddy shoots back.

"Daddy." I'm done with this bullshit.

"With respect, *Bill*, your rules suck," Iverson says flatly.

Daddy's face turns redder. "Don't call me Bill. You will respect me in my place of business."

"Why?" Iverson asks. "You're not respecting me. And you're not respecting her."

I blink at Iverson. He's not just sticking up for himself and his brothers. He's trying to advocate for me.

Daddy blusters. "I know what's best for her and this ranch, and it's not you."

"You're not the only one who wants what's best for her." Iverson narrows his eyes. "You'd lose three employees over this?"

Daddy stalks closer. "Listen—"

"I quit." I straighten and lift my chin.

Daddy takes a breath like he's going to keep speaking, and then he stops and shakes his head. "What?"

Iverson peers at me, astonishment scrawled across his face.

"I'm done, Daddy. You're overstepping, and I can't have it."

"You'd quit because of me?" Iverson asks softly.

I nod, captured in the beam of his stunned brown gaze. "Yes. I like you, Iverson. A lot. I want more, and I hope you do too." My shoulders hang. "I should've done this before I cost you and your brothers your jobs."

"You didn't cost us our jobs. Your dad and his need for control did." Iverson's smirk lacks humor. "But I'm not the rancher who's going into the fall and winter short three experienced employees."

"Jamison." Fear laces Daddy's voice. "You're not quitting."

"Yes, I am." I hold Iverson's warm gaze. "And I'm moving." I switch my attention to Daddy. My chest constricts. The hurt in his face guts me, but I have to do this. "Not anywhere on Hawthorne land either."

He recoils. "I've already talked to the builder—"

"Exactly, Daddy. I've asked you repeatedly to stay out of my house-hunting efforts." I throw my arms out. "It's too much. I want my own life. I'll always appreciate everything you and Mom have done for me, but I'm my own person."

"You'll quit over *him*?"

"Yes, but also, I'm quitting for me. You won't respect my boundaries as your daughter or as your employee."

My pulse jackhammers. I'm in over my head. I quit my job over a man. I might've gotten to this point eventually, but between Iverson and this office, my choice is clear. Yet I don't know if I martyred myself for a reason other than independence. Will I be looking for a job and a place to live as a single woman?

I chance a peek at Iverson, but his expression is full of shock and dismay. Is that pride in his eyes or wishful thinking?

"You're making pretty big decisions for a guy you've just met," Daddy warns. "I think you need to slow down and think about things. You don't know Hennessy. You have no idea if he's even a good man or not."

Iverson pivots to face Daddy. "You know what kind of man I am." His tone is even, almost dangerous. Daddy insulted him.

Daddy holds a hand up. "I know you're a good employee. I haven't heard about you sleeping around, but I know you ain't abstinent."

"That's my point. You've assumed what I'm like. I could've had a different woman every night, and that would've stopped as soon as I met Sunny. It's only been her since I met her, and it'll always be just her. I am a good man, William. And your daughter makes me want to be a better one. Just so happens, my brothers and I were ready to put in our notice. Only we were going to be considerate and offer to stay long enough to train the new people in. Guess I don't have to worry about that."

My heart leaps, knocking my guilt back. He was planning to quit too? All three of them?

I slip my hand through his, afraid he'll walk out and leave me behind. "You were going to quit?"

"Sunny, I'm dying to take you on a date. I want to show off the woman I'm wild about."

It's amazing I don't melt into the floor. "You do?"

"And if I have to quit to do it, that's what I'm going to do." He tips my chin up. "But I'm not a man without a plan."

I'm distantly aware of Daddy watching us, but Iverson is the center of my world.

"What you said about land management not being straight buy or sell stuck with me," Iverson continues, ignoring Daddy. "I talked to the guys, and we're all ready for something different. For more. So I did some research, I talked to Myles Foster, and we're doing more." He grins, delight radiating off him. "You're looking at one of the investors of the next Foster House distillery. Not only that, I'm going to be learning how to run the place and make some damn good whiskey."

He sounds so excited and proud. I clutch his hands and jump up and down. "Seriously?"

He laughs. "I'm almost as excited as Durban. He's been figuring out how to become a master distiller."

"You're sure about all this?" He's not making changes for me, but I feel responsible.

"It's time." He strokes a hand down my face. "We knew we didn't want to sell, but we weren't sure what to do or how to use our dad's land in a way that'd help us and honor him." He tips his forehead closer to mine. "You really want to keep me around?"

"I really do." I stand on my tiptoes to bring my mouth closer to his.

Daddy clears his throat, but I don't pull back. I plant a kiss firmly on Iverson's lips.

Daddy clears his throat again. "Can we talk about this?"

"I think we're done talking, Daddy." I'm ready to get Iverson to myself and not have to hide it.

"There's no need to rush off." My dad shifts his weight. His brows are drawn, and his mouth is in a troubled line.

I grip Iverson's hand tighter. "I have a date that's long past due, Daddy. I'm going to grab my things from the house and then take my boyfriend out to lunch."

"Not if your boyfriend takes you out first," Iverson growls. He cocks his elbow out and hooks my hand through it. Then he stuffs his hat on his head and dips the brim at Daddy. "Mr. Hawthorne. I'll let you know where to send those checks."

Iverson

One year later...

I'm in the parking lot of the mine that's slowly being turned into a distillery. The crew started on the inside, making sure the structure's safe. Two months ago, the exterior remodeling and reconstruction began.

Myles Foster's next to me, squinting at the progress. Since we're only a couple of hours from Bourbon Canyon, we've met up often. He's been dressed down each visit compared to the first time I met him. His worn jeans look like they've seen some hard work, but he wears a black polo with the yellow Foster House logo. His brothers, Lane and Cruz, are with him, dressed the same.

Apparently, the two younger Foster guys' paths weren't much different than mine and my brothers'. They started working on the Bailey ranch until they were mentored at the original Foster House for several years, learning the ropes. They're younger than my brothers, with Cruz being the youngest of us all. Both guys are down-to-earth and easygoing.

My brothers checked in before going to the river to fish. I stayed behind. I have plans later.

"We'll be ready to start the first batch next spring," Myles says. "The rest of the area looks good." He crosses his arms. "I see they finally broke ground on the northeast corner of the rickhouse."

I nod. "Foundation's going in this week."

He slaps my shoulder. "Can't wait to see the place."

He checks his watch. "I gotta head out. I'm on swimming lesson duty tonight. Keep me updated."

I'm in charge of the remodel. Myles hired me as the project manager since I know the local contractors or I know someone who knows someone. I couldn't date any of the guests when I worked at Hawthorne Ranch, but that never stopped me from talking to people and making connections.

My brothers are already working too. All three of us rolled up our sleeves and waded in. The work is hard, but it'll be worth it. In the meantime, we're learning as much as we can about the distilling world and periodically traveling to Denver to train at Foster House.

Myles is about to get into his pickup when I say, "Hey, man. Thanks again."

I'm not a businessman, or at least I wasn't, but I know that Myles didn't have to do what he did. He didn't have to negotiate with me. He didn't have to take on my brothers. And he didn't have to sign over part of his empire to us. He has enough money to buy and build wherever he wants. He can fire people and make sure he's the only one at the top. Instead, he's widening his circle. To be a part of it, we sold off a portion of the land with the mine and used the money to invest in Foster House Gold, what Myles decided to call the Huckleberry Springs portion of his empire. The rest of the land was split into three, a section each for me, Durban, and Haven. We already have some cattle and decided to ranch together too.

I told Sunny once that I wanted to learn something new, and it's like a firehose of info is blasting me. Myles's brothers think they can make some damn good gin and vodka. My brothers got just as excited talking with them about it, so Myles met with me. He thought pivoting and offering other spirits was the way to go with the Huckleberry Springs site. I agreed because fuck it. I'll do anything. The future is wide open.

"No need to thank me." Myles sweeps his gaze over the property. "Darin Bailey always said, 'Don't get so stuck in your lane you can't see a better path.'" He lifts his chin toward the distillery in the making. "This is a better lane. Have a good night. Get home to that wife of yours."

That's one rule I'll follow. Someday, I'll be like him.

No. I'll have my own story. I've only just started writing it.

I get in my pickup and head to town. I make one stop before I pull in front of a small one-story house. It's old. A fixer-upper, and that's what I've been doing.

Thanks to the deal with Myles, my brothers and I had a little left over after investing with Foster House Gold. I had enough left to help us get by until construction on my house begins. Until then, I've worked on this house to flip. My brothers also bought a house together to remodel and sell. Eventually, Durban will build like Sunny and I are doing, and Haven's going to remodel our childhood home.

Inside, I toss a meatloaf in the oven. Just as I straighten, the front door opens.

"Hey, baby," I call.

"Hey." Sunny breezes in. Her dress today is full of daisies, and I already cornered her before work and flipped the hem up to plunge inside.

She beelines right to me, and I sweep her into my arms. After a kiss that could turn into another quickie before dinner, I set her down and drop to my knees. There's one more greeting I need to make.

I spread my hands over her rounded stomach and kiss it through the fabric. "How's my little one doing?"

"She's doing jumping jacks on my bladder."

Sunny and I married last fall in a little ceremony on the Hawthorne ranch. She and I insisted the reception take place at the guesthouse and that everyone be invited.

After we both quit—technically, I got fired—William finally persuaded Sunny and me to hear him out. He wanted her to keep working for him. The ranch was her home, and she loved the business. She took the deal and remodeled her office. He also wanted her to keep living with him, but she and I had found this place on that first lunch date.

In the last year, I've gone from bachelor hired help to a husband, a homeowner, and a partial business owner. Next, I'll be a dad.

Goddamn. My chest grows tight. I make sure every day that Sunny is as happy and content as she makes me. She likes working for Hawthorne Ranch, and she fucking loves me. Her parents have gotten over their reservations about me, and they like me now too. William's still a little salty about Haven and Durban, but it's likely because he blames himself for losing all three of us.

I rise and go to the fridge. I withdraw a small box. "I got something for you."

"You spoil me."

"It's because I love you so much."

"And I love you." With a grin, she snatches the box out of my hand and opens the lid. "Ooh, she added chocolate-covered almonds today." She plucks one of the chocolate-covered strawberries out and takes a bite.

Her eyes roll back, and she moans. "I've been craving these all day."

The strawberries are her go-to craving. I make sure she stays well stocked. Elodie jokes that she'll have to name her first kid after Sunny as a thank-you for all the business. Her version of a thank-you is to add some little surprise for Sunny to each box I buy.

After she finishes chewing, she bites her bottom lip like she wants to say something.

"You know you can tell me anything," I say. We've been as open with each other as that first night in the cab of my truck.

"Campbell wants to come for a visit."

"You make it sound like that's a problem." Her youngest—and most precocious—sister. Campbell Hawthorne is responsibility adverse, perpetually late, and that included her arrival to our wedding, but she's got a big heart and she loves her family.

"I'd like to have everyone over before the baby comes, but I know how she gets on Durban's nerves."

"He can deal." I was worried about meeting Jamison's sisters and being judged as not good enough. Both sisters embraced me and my brothers. Haven's cool with both of them. Durban and the middle sister, Avery, get along, but they're the most alike. Durban and Campbell are oil and water. Thankfully, they don't often have to mix. When they do, Durban just grinds his teeth and ignores her. "We all like your family, every single one, and even any annoying ones. They've accepted us, and we accept them. You don't know how much that means to guys who've lost their family and their home."

Her sweet smile lights up my entire day. I twirl her around so I can bury my nose at the nape of her neck. My hands rest on the baby, who will be here in four months. "I've also had my own cravings today."

"You seem to have that craving a lot." I can hear the smile in her voice.

"I'm a hungry man, Mrs. Hennessy." I never get tired of calling her that. I'm a fucking caveman around her, and I don't care.

"Well, Mr. Hennessy. What are we going to do about that?"

I drag up her skirt. "I have some ideas."

"They'd better not include the parking lot at the mine."

I chuckle. "No. I'm not risking anyone getting a look at what's mine." After the sale, security cameras were set up.

She sets the box of strawberries on the counter and spins around. "I'm really proud of you. I love you, but I love seeing you and your brothers embark on this adventure."

I owed them. That night at the bar, they'd helped me figure this life out. They'd done just as much research as me, and it wasn't just because they were ready for a change. They could see how crazy I was about Sunny. "You made it all possible."

"You three were the spark. I was just a little breeze." She twines her arms around my neck. "The real work is being done by you, Haven, and Durban. I'm proud of all of you. But I'm especially fond of my very own whiskey cowboy."

. . .

Campbell Hawthorne is ready to prove herself, but she gets tipsy instead, and ends up puking on the most uptight Hennessy's boots. But when Durban learns she let loose because she's going to be tied up planning her ex's wedding—to her cousin—for the next month, he decides to help her. He'll show Campbell that the best way to relax is a smooth whiskey and a hot cowboy in Whiskey Bargain.

You're invited to Iverson and Sunny's wedding! You might get to see when Campbell first starts getting under Durban's collar in a special bonus epilogue at walkerrosebooks.com/bonus-content/

9 781951 067816